Tango With Me

Tango With Me

A Migrant's Romance Book 2: Argentina

Ana Dantra

Dedication

To the Argentinean matriarchs I've met along the way. To their wit, their kindness, and their strength. To all the functional medicine warrior, who actually risk their skin to honor their vows.

Acknowledgments

This book is the result of a team work, a joint effort to make it the best version of itself. Russell, thanks for taking the time to read, proofread and get under the characters' skin. Without you, Rob wouldn't be who he is. You gave a male voice to the male characters, something really hard for me to grasp. You came up with full situations that added richness to the story. I can't thank you enough. Kathryn, I know how busy you are, how hard it is to take time from an already impossible schedule to edit, comb and fix all my prepositional messes and weird expressions. Thank you. You are not only a brilliant writer and a dedicated editor, you are one of the kindest persons I've ever met.

Chapter 1

Rob

Tapping rhythmically with his gold and silver Mont Blanc pen on the maple-colored desk, Doctor Robert MacArthur reclined in his office chair and took a deep breath. *This is good.* The name on the top left of the results sheet read W. T. Humphrey, and the content showed his lifelong friend had recovered his iron health in record time. *Only a nerd can get all warm and fuzzy over some numbers.* His eyes became misty and the corner of his lips pulled up into a smile.

The phone beeped and his stomach growled almost at the same time. A glance at the Twitter feed of his favorite food truck showed it was nearby. *Just two blocks away.* He would have to hurry if he wanted to catch it. His eyes drifted toward the pile of papers stacked on the desk and rocketed back to the Twitter feed. *Darn, this is important.* As if on cue, his stomach growled again.

A quick knock on the door led immediately to the knob twisting followed by his secretary's head peeking out from the side of the metal frame.

"The truck is coming, let's go!" Alice said eagerly.

"I can't. You go." A gush of air rushed theatrically out of his lungs.

"What do you mean you can't? It's the food truck!"

The twenty-two-year-old girl was a ray of sunshine, quite literally as her blonde hair reflected the light wherever she went. Rob loved to take his lunch break with her and hear all the gossip of the office, especially on sunny, windy days when she became, unknowingly, a piece of art in her own right.

"Sometimes I work, you know?"

"I know how hard you work." Her delicate face softened even more. "I'll bring you a schnitzel, but only this time so you don't get ideas about becoming an obnoxious boss on me."

"I wouldn't dare," Rob answered, grinning.

She wrinkled her nose at him and closed the door.

* * *

The office was a pompous display of intent put at the service of distaste. Behind a replica of Napoleon's desk, sat Roger Leven, the clinic's vice-president, dwarfed inside a huge tufted leather armchair. On the further wall behind him, a hand-painted replica of the Mona Lisa three times its real size was encased in a convoluted golden frame. *If you could talk, lady.* The art on the side walls was more modern and a lot more disturbing. "Gods of the Modern World," read the caption under a picture of skeletons dressed in leadership garments. It had been positioned right by a huge window. The opposite wall displayed a three-panel image of a very realistic bald eagle ready to attack.

"Please, take a seat."

Rob pulled the meeting room chair forward and crouched on it as best as he could. It was lime green and designed for a far smaller frame than his. He realized the whole setup was purposely chosen to make any normal-sized male feel extremely uncomfortable. *Roger's torture chamber, how fun.* No wonder most meetings took place at the conference room.

"So, do you have numbers to show me?"

"Yes," answered Rob, pushing forward a pile of papers with graphics. "I separated my patients into two groups, one changed to the new protocols and the second one stayed the same."

"You did what?" The small and hard eyes of the man looked at Rob over the metal frame of his glasses as if he were about to pounce.

This doesn't look good...

"It was completely consensual. I offered the new protocols. Some took them, some didn't. The ones that did signed the corresponding agreements. This gave me the chance to compare results over similar enough cases."

"It's not a double-blind study. It has no scientific value," the short man interrupted with contempt.

"Well..." Rob tried to reason, understanding that at this point, there was no possible meeting of minds, "if you dig deep enough into the science, you realize that the double-blind has no definite value either. It's just a reasonable working agreement, that's all. In some cases of vital importance, like vaccines, for example, there are no double-blind studies done at all."

Roger huffed. "You know it's not done because it would be inhumane for the placebo cases."

"Of course. I'm just stating a fact."

"So, what are these curves supposed to show me?" Roger grunted.

"That functional medicine protocols are on average three times more efficient than the regular ones—at least with my patients."

Roger took a deep breath, grabbed a Kleenex from his drawer and cleaned his lenses thoroughly.

"Of all the doctors in the clinic, Robert, you are the one I least expected to see bringing this nonsense up."

Now *that* was an interesting statement.

"What do you mean?" Rob tilted his head.

"You come from a family that understands success in business. Didn't you have any training at all?"

"Of course I did." Rob remembered each one of the business trainings he'd attended; some rendered better memories than others.

"Then why did you bring these papers to me when you should have brought a business plan showing how these changes will increase the cash flow of the clinic?"

Rob was about to answer when Roger stopped him by lifting his index finger. He put both elbows on the desk and pushed his stout body forward.

"I'll tell you why: because it's not possible! First: there is no insurance coverage for these procedures, so we would be subject to liability and we could only take cash clients. Second: it reduces recurring business drastically. Third: we would have to reinvent our partner network. Fourth: we would have to refinance via bank loan the construction your father is building for us when right now we have zero interest for fifteen years. We're talking about millions and millions of dollars in losses. Your proposal would bankrupt us! Is that what you want?"

Rob looked at Miss Mona Lisa behind Roger's shoulder, her smile more secretive than ever. *If you could talk, lady.* He sighed and scratched the back of his neck.

"I'm talking about life and death and you answer with cash flow issues. I thought we were in the health business, with *health* being the *keyword.*"

The small man waved his hand as if there was a fly in front of him.

"And we are. But for any business, its own survival is the bottom line. We're saving lives already. Think how many would suffer if we go out of business."

"But..."

"No buts. Find a way to make it profitable, and we'll consider it. Now, if you excuse me, I have another appointment right... about... now," he said, looking at his bulky Swiss wristwatch.

Roger's phone beeped, and the door opened.

Rob turned right in time to see the long legs of Millicent Pearson making an appearance, ending in her signature five inches heels. She wore a short tight pencil skirt and a low-cut white silk blouse under an almost professional looking business jacket. The woman looked as bony and bitchy as he remembered. Well... maybe even more. Rob shivered at the sight of those heels. He still had nightmares about the witch's shoe sole pressing his throat and cutting off the airflow.

"Robert MacArthur. What a pleasant surprise." Her lips curled in a predatory smile.

Rob stood fast, almost tumbling the chair to the floor.

"Ms. Pearson," he nodded and turned his attention to Roger who had also stood up and was looking at the woman with adoring puppy dog eyes. *Holy shit…* "Roger, I'll see what I can do about those numbers," he said as he hurried to the door.

"You do that," the man whispered, but his attention was not on Rob anymore.

Chapter 2

Alejandra

The ghostly shadows of the night loomed over the woman at the door of the small pub. *He's not coming.*

"Your man's late again?" Alejandra's tango partner, Fermin, pressed his shoulder to the wall of the dark corridor and lit a joint.

Her eyes closed into two slits of pure contempt. The performance tonight had been very spirited, *too* spirited. She hated to be taken advantage of, and that's exactly what he'd done. Alejandra was almost glad her boyfriend hadn't made it. It would've ended badly.

"He probably had an emergency and please don't smoke that stuff close to me."

"Have you ever tried it?" Fermin blew the thick, spicy air directly at her face, a smirk pulling at the seam of his lips and his sunken, tiny eyes gleaming.

Her back straightened, her head slanted, and a smug smile mimicked his posture.

"I have. When assholes like you choose to smoke in public and I get it second hand. I hate it when it happens."

"Ouch. That was harsh." The slim man crouched as if he had received a blow.

She folded her arms in front of her chest and lifted her chin defiantly. "Not killing that shit when I politely asked you was harsh. This is just my reaction."

His fingers opened, letting the twisted cigarette fall on the floor, where it was thoroughly crushed by the sole of his impeccable patent-leather shoe.

"So… have you thought about the trip?"

"I'm still thinking about it. My brother took the contract to an attorney and he said it looked fine, except for the visa issue."

"I told you it was a lot faster this way. That's the only reason."

She felt his anger rising and mimicked it with one of her own. "Yes, but a tourist visa is granted to spend money, not to work. Dancing for profit would be illegal."

His body entered her personal space and she recoiled. They'd been dancing together for three years and they were pure passion on the dance floor, but she couldn't stand his proximity away from the stage. There was something about him that repelled her. If only she could find another dancer as good as him, but nicer. It seemed that the really good ones were all taken.

"The company does this all the time with different performers around the world. They know their business, Alejandra. It's Broadway we're talking about!"

A heartfelt sigh escaped her lungs, as her palm pushed his chest softly away to a manageable distance. It was too late, and she was too tired to have this conversation. "I haven't made up my mind yet."

His lips made a tsk sound.

"Well, I hate to hurry you, but I'm not missing out on this opportunity. You have till Friday."

"What's that supposed to mean?"

Fermin's long fingers brushed the stubble on his pointy chin. "You know what it means…"

Without saying another word, the man brushed by her and walked into the night of Buenos Aires.

Alejandra sighed again, pulled out her phone and called a cab.

* * *

There were spiders inside an empty toilet. Crouched down naked in front of it, she wrapped a cloth around the seat and observed them. Alejandra didn't fear them, as she'd allowed them to be there, but now her plans had changed. She'd managed to take one of the spiders out of the toilet with a short wooden stick, but there were still two more to go when a voice intruded in her dream.

"Ale, wake up. Pablo's here."

A leg escaping from a crumpled purple comforter, her arms hugging a big pillow, the young woman opened her eyes reluctantly. Bright lines of light painted the yellow curtains with lively gold and spread along the dim chamber toward the white side table and matching drawer. She was in her bedroom.

"Mom? What time is it?" she mumbled through parched lips.

"Nine thirty," her mother's voice came clear from the other side of the door.

"It's too early…" She turned, wrapping her legs around the comforter and trying to go back to sleep.

The door opened and Nydia entered without further preamble. Her porcelain skin and bright brown eyes didn't match the abundant grey strands that populated her otherwise black, nicely-bobbed hair.

"No. For normal people, it isn't. Now, get up," she said, hands on hips and a smile dancing on her face.

Alejandra reluctantly sat up on the bed and looked at the natural result of her tumultuous lifestyle. Her dress hung from the back of a chair, makeup and combs lay scattered on her dresser, and the big mirror reflected shoes and discarded clothing lying all around.

"Alright, I'm coming…" she whined.

Nydia chuckled, turned on her heels and left, closing the door softly behind her.

Alejandra fished for something to wear distractedly, thinking what kind of apology Pablo would pull this time. *He probably had an emergency. Maybe he is cheating on me… Nah.* Dressed in a tank top, a pair of jeans and tennis shoes, the girl in the mirror looked completely different from the femme-fatale of the night before. Like day and night. A messy ponytail and just a shadow of lip gloss were all she'd done to her face at this time, giving her the fresh look of a teenager.

"If you're going to wake me up at sunrise, at least take me to a nice place for breakfast," she told her boyfriend after a quick peck on his lips. He just smiled and offered his palm to her.

Hand in hand, they walked the two blocks to Rapanui, a chocolate shop slash ice cream parlor slash coffee place, which was one of Alejandra's favorite places in the whole world.

"Welsh cake and coffee?"

"Yes!" She nodded emphatically while taking a seat at her favorite table outside. Funny enough, this cake wasn't a Welsh typical food. It was a recipe from a Welsh family who arrived in Patagonia in the late nineteen century. A dark cake with rich flavor due to brown sugar, honey, nuts and candied fruit, it was famous for having several months of shelf-life.

Adoringly, Alejandra watched the man playing juggler with her food and his. Six years together, pretty much all her twenties. Who would have guessed? Not her. He was the worst dancer she'd ever seen, a hopeless case, yet his honesty and kindness had won her heart. They were just waiting for him to finish his residency to move in together. Of course, their parents wanted them to get married, but they didn't want to go through that particular mess. Not yet anyway.

"What happened last night?" she asked, as soon as the coffee did its magic.

His brown eyes were sunken, making his aquiline nose even more prominent. He pulled his straight, dark blond hair away from his forehead and sighed.

"We delivered a baby at eleven, but there were complications. The cord was around the neck. It turned out all right, thank God, but we sweated bullets for two hours. I decided to take a nap before picking you up and didn't hear the alarm. I was too tired. I'm really sorry."

"It's not your fault." Alejandra took his hand to comfort him.

He sighed deeply. "Do you feel it too?"

"What?"

"That our lives are pushing us apart?"

Her eyes turned foggy and she nodded a couple of times.

"Are you cheating on me?" she asked, after playing with her food for twelve long breaths.

"No. You?"

"Of course not!"

Pablo interlocked their fingers, reclined in the bar's armchair and closed his eyes. He looked physically and emotionally exhausted. The eye bags had a dark hue, and his skin was sickly white. He'd just ended a forty-eight-hour shift at one of the busiest hospitals in a city with three million people, but instead of being sleeping, he was here.

Alejandra knew something would have to change, but she felt trapped. She remembered her dream and an absurd idea formed: Maybe if she'd managed to take the other two spiders out of the toilet, everything would be fine.

"Look, if we are going to make it work, live together, get married, some things will have to change."

"What do you mean?" All of a sudden, she was not hungry anymore.

"I want you to stop performing at night. Keep the tango classes in the evening. Maybe you can teach ballet to children in the morning, but I can't be worrying about your safety or about that pervert grabbing your ass while I'm delivering a new life. I need to think clearly, but I can't."

Sicilian heat rising, Alejandra stared at him. He wanted her to leave the spotlight for good? Just like that? And spend her nights alone? Waiting for him?

"You don't know what you're asking. I am the way I am because of performing. Like most artists, I live for the applause. If I left it all and stayed home… I'd be a needy bundle of nerves calling you every five minutes just to hear your voice."

"You don't know that." He sat straight, a clear plea in his eyes.

"I don't, but that's how I feel it will be," she murmured, her own eyes tearful.

"So, what do we do?" There was love, tenderness, but also deep exhaustion in his voice.

"I don't know…" her words came out broken.

She really didn't know. She loved Pablo with all her heart. Except for dancing, he was everything she wanted in a man. He was kind, loving, had a purpose in life that was bigger than himself, yet things had changed. Their lives were palpably pushing them apart, and passion was fading. They hadn't made love in how long? Two, three months? They weren't even married for goodness sake!

Performing was her own small way to make this world a better place. She might not save lives, but she was making people happy, helping them connect with their own spirits. She would be fine performing in a small place, maybe only on the weekends, yet he was asking her to leave it all, so… evidently, he didn't see any value in what she did.

Alejandra was one with her art. If he didn't care for it, did he care for her at all?

She needed her man to love all of her back. Was it even possible?

He took her hand to his lips and kissed her knuckles.

"I love you, baby," he murmured.

"I love you too," Alejandra sobbed.

Chapter 3

Rob

Sheltering his eyes from the sun's reflection on the surf, Rob studied their destination. The day was glorious, with a soft breeze and small clouds flying lazily on the deep, light-blue sky. Yet it was hard to enjoy when they were rushing toward their own demise at dazzling speed.

"Hey, Dad, don't you think we're too close to land?" he yelled toward the bridge of the boat when the knot in his stomach became unbearable.

His father didn't answer but maneuvered the boat and dropped anchor.

"How many times have we been in Sand City?" the old man asked, after climbing down from the bridge, his thick eyebrows furrowed.

"Many."

"And you are still afraid? Haven't you studied the charts?"

Rob reined back his temper. This side of the tongue of sand dropped fast into deep waters, which was one of the main assets of this otherwise bland location. Still, they were dangerously close and they both knew it. His father seemed determined to use him as an emotional punching bag today. *Go figure.*

"I still think we're too close," he quipped as lightheartedly as he could manage, images of wreckage and sharks still attacking from the back of his mind.

"That's because you're a fucking pussy!" The veins in the old man's neck were thick and his cheeks flushed.

What was it with his father today?

Rob's training kicked in. What could he use as a defibrillator in case of a heart attack? *Not much.* What to do? Divert. Calm him down. Make him laugh. *Yeah right.*

The young man put on his favorite clown face. "Alright, so you brought me all the way to nowhere to insult me? Couldn't you just text?"

The old man huffed.

"We're not in the middle of nowhere. We're inside Huntington Bay. Right at home, so to speak." He squared his shoulders and crossed his arms in front of his chest, determined to keep his fighting stance going.

"I'll go get the fishing gear," Rob said, hoping to find a place to hide.

"No need. Just bring a couple of beers from the fridge. We need to talk."

Rob's forehead wrinkled. *This can't be good.*

Placing the beers on a folding table that had appeared in the middle of the deck, Rob sat on the only empty chair. The second one cradled the heavy bulk of his father, who was looking at some photos. Rob knew that expression very well. In his childhood, it was usually followed by his father backhanding him with enough force to make him fall. It didn't happen too often, just enough to remember.

But Rob was not a small child anymore.

"So, are you going to hit me now or later?" he asked nonchalantly.

The man finally controlled his anger, but instead of just sighing and relaxing, he became cold as stone. Rob had seen this too, but never toward him. It was more disconcerting and scarier than his father's furious face. This meant business.

"With deep sorrow, I've come to finally accept that you are not a MacArthur. You look like one, but you're just not, and this is why I'm disinheriting you. By tomorrow, you need to vacate the apartment and deliver the car keys to the Manhattan office."

Rob stood frozen as if he had received a heavy blow. It was not the prospect of being homeless and broke that really worried him. He'd never had a day of lack in his life, so he had no idea what it meant. But to be rejected by his own father like this... They never got along, ever, but they were family... or so he thought.

The young man nodded a couple of times and took a swing of his beer. It was a supermarket brand, one of the really cheap ones. He almost spat it out. "God, Father... this is foul-tasting!"

His father smirked. "Get used to it. It's all *you* can afford with *your* income and *your* expenses..."

Rob felt like a gruff teenager all over again, scolded and threatened after doing something *terrible*, like skinny-dipping in the family pool with some friends after a party.

"Why are you doing this? What did I do this time that got you all worked up?" he asked with a grumpy, whiny voice that revealed his state of mind.

The old man sighed and shook his head a couple of times. All of a sudden, he looked very old and very tired.

"Roger Leven called me yesterday. They're about to fire you and sue you *and MacArthur Enterprises* for a hundred million dollars. They're also about to cancel the construction of their new clinic downtown. Their lenders and partners, the pharmaceutical Bymax LLC, threatened to terminate their agreements due to a breach of contract. Apparently, they found out you've been practicing *witchcraft*, instead of using the pertinent protocols."

"Witchcraft? What the hell? How did all that happen?"

"*You* tell *me*. All I know is that your stupidity is flushing the whole family and everything I built these past thirty years down the drain. If I have to, I *will* cut you loose. Saving the deal cost me dearly already. But you... I don't know what to do to set you straight, with one exception..."

"Which is?" Rob was sure it was not going to be fun.

"You'll need to get married."

"What?"

"And not to any woman. You need one who can manage your *rarities* and who has a good business head on her shoulders. And I have the right lady for you. The name is Millicent Pearson." The old man gave his son a picture. From the color-rich paper, a very hot, and fully malignant Millicent scantily dressed in dom gear smirked at him.

Rob gulped.

"Father… this woman is a total psycho."

"Marry her, and I also give you a small clinic to practice your witchcraft," his father pressed.

"I just can't. Do you really think this bitch can become a wife?"

"I think she's perfect for a broke-ass faggot like you. She'll make you walk straight again," the old man added, pushing forward yet another pair of images, this time of Rob in leather, whipping a guy tied to a Saint Andrew's cross into orgasm.

"This…" his father said, stabbing the image with his index finger "is not a MacArthur. You're a disgrace."

The old man had tears in his eyes when he suddenly got up and walked toward the bridge, raised the anchor, turned the engine on and headed back to port.

Chapter 4

Alejandra

Arriving at La Guardia didn't bring a sensation of butterflies, but rather of impending doom. This trip hadn't been her dream. It'd been a desperate move to stay afloat amidst her desolation.

Pablo had seen a photo with Fermin's hand way up her parts during that fatidic performance and decided he'd had enough. Not only that, he broke their six-year relationship by kissing a blonde in front of her face. It was so... humiliating.

She'd seen it coming. Yet, it felt as if the rug that was her life had been pulled out from under her feet. So she'd looked at her options and traveling didn't look so bad, dangers and all, *Fermin and all.*

Alejandra stared out the plane's window as it came to a stop. This was great, right? Then why was she so worried?

Fermin, on the other hand, was exultant.

"New York," he said with his small black eyes bright as he fidgeted in his seat like a small child after eating candy. "We are going to make it big!"

He turned Alejandra's head and pecked her lips, taking her completely by surprise.

"What are you doing?"

He just shrugged and gave her an impish smile.

"Don't do that again."

"Uh-huh…"

"I mean it!"

He chuckled.

"Goodness. You are impossible."

"C'mon, sweets. Don't you feel it? The promised land awaits us." He took a deep breath and a beatific smile arched his lips. "You and me, together. Success is inevitable."

Alejandra sighed. *If only…*

The line for customs was long, but it moved fast. Fermin showed his passport first.

"Chile, hum?"

"Yes, ma'am," he said, grinning.

"You have a visa waiver, which means you can stay for only three months. What brings you here?"

The woman observed him carefully, her eyes scanning him up and down.

He looked like those men who would easily stay illegally. If he had applied for a visa, he probably wouldn't have got one.

"Broadway," he said. "We have tickets for Hamilton." Fermin smiled brightly and showed a couple of tickets Alejandra didn't even know existed in the first place.

The woman looked briefly at Alejandra.

"Lucky you. They sell out for the whole year in days. What hotel are you staying in?"

"Casablanca. Right in Times Square. Here are the reservations."

She nodded a couple of times, checking the papers.

"Nice. Please, place the four fingers of your right hand in this screen, then the thumb. Same for the other hand. Look at the camera… The lady comes with you?"

"Yes," he answered. "The love of my life…" he said and stamped a kiss on Alejandra's cheek, making her fume—and enjoying every minute of it.

"Passport, please?"

Alejandra gave her the passport with shaky hands and the woman checked the details.

"Argentina?"

Alejandra nodded.

"This is not your first trip..."

"No, I came to Disney when I was fifteen. It was a full package with a cruise."

The woman looked at her, back at Fermin and nodded a couple of times.

"Same procedure, please." She looked intently as Alejandra's information showed on a screen. "Everything looks in order. You could stay up to six months with this visa, but as your partner can only be three, I'll give you three months as well," said the woman. She stamped both passports before giving them back.

"I didn't know you were Chilean..." Alejandra commented when they were far enough.

He just winked.

On the other side of the arrivals door, a bulky man with a two-day beard awaited them. He assessed her up and down with lecherous eyes, making her feel like merchandise.

"Where are we going?" Alejandra asked as soon as she noticed they were not heading downtown.

"Work," the man grunted.

Alejandra contained the urge to groan. She was jet-lagged and deathly tired. All she wanted right now was a hot shower and a bed.

Fermin turned from the front seat and looked at her excitedly. "We are dancing tonight!"

Alejandra curled up in a ball in the back seat and tried to catch some sleep.

* * *

The stage was low and circular. Alejandra knew there were tables all around it, but at this time the illumination was so focused on the platform that she almost couldn't discern them. She could see the next step, her partner, and hardly anything else. Yet she could feel eyes on her. *Predatory eyes.*

They'd prepared a performance with tango and rumba on the second part, with the help of Manuel, a Cuban guy who was the most fluid dancer she'd ever seen. She loved his energy and his passion, and the fact that he only had eyes for Fermin during the breaks. She found it refreshing.

This presentation was a closed one for high-tier members of a private club and would second as publicity spot for their show. She had to sign a contract giving away the rights to the recording and a non-disclosure agreement, which made her feel *very uneasy.*

The music started and Alejandra entered *the zone.* It was a state of fluidity and surrender that made her into a willing puppet of her partner. Fermin was an amazing dancer, and she was complete putty in his hands. Her dance partner took her in a succession of fast tango paces called eights and scissors, which pushed her to her breath limit and made her feel lightheaded. She forgot the very improper clothes, she forgot the exaggerated makeup, she almost forgot that they had forced her into submitting to a full body wax a couple of hours before. Almost. Some parts were still tender.

Fermin slowed down as the music evolved from the two by four of tango into the vivid rhythm of rumba. Manuel came to the floor and placed himself at her back. Fermin made her turn and delivered her into Manuel's arms. His hands were strong and warm. Fermin kept his own hands on her waist and guided the trio through the dance floor.

Alejandra was completely out of herself. Fermin covered her eyes with a silk handkerchief. This was not part of the routine, but she found darkness welcoming. There was no stage or audience, just her, the music and her two partners. The men sandwiched her closer and the rhythm transmuted again into something closer to a bachata. She was getting hot. So hot. She surrendered to the feelings and the music. Her body became even more elastic and supple.

That was until another hand feather-lightly touched the side of her breast, and some of her alarms went off. A third man? This was not part of the routine they'd rehearsed either.

She inhaled sharply and could catch a whiff of a different cologne mixed with alcohol.

All of a sudden, the darkness became oppressive. The feeling of that touch cut the flow of the dance. Manuel pulled her knee upwards and she became completely extended and exposed. Fermin's hands were firm on her waist, keeping her in place.

Something brushed her inner thigh, and Alejandra jumped. This new man... wasn't even a dancer. His timing was completely wrong. *Game over.*

Her body decided way before her mind to stop this—whatever *this* was. She suddenly swirled in a ballet step that took her companions by surprise and allowed her to move away from the trio and the spotlight. Alejandra stripped the handkerchief away from her eyes and what she saw drained the blood away from her face. There were eight naked men, of all colors, sizes and ages, with their members erect and apparently ready to take their share.

Alejandra didn't wait another second. She turned toward the corridor they had come from and ran for her life.

The two closest guys cut off her escape, while Fermin desperately tried to grab her arm. Thank goodness she was oiled from head to toe and slipped from his grasp. Manuel was nearby but didn't try to get her. When she looked at him, he winked. Alejandra smiled briefly and charged toward the guys blocking the entrance. She squeezed herself between them by making a jump that landed in a tumble. She rolled up and kept running.

Instead of heading toward the door, she went to the dressing room. On a hunch, she'd hidden her passport and credit cards in a cleaning closet nearby. It was probably very dumb, but she couldn't stand the idea of being at the docks of a foreign country without identity and without her credit cards, with nobody to call for help.

Opening the closet door, she found a man and a woman putting small trash bags into a bigger bag. The girl was young and beautiful, with a heart-shaped face. The guy seemed to be in his thirties, going on twelve. Tall and goofy, he looked harmless enough.

"Sorry to interrupt, guys. I just need…"

The girl pulled Alejandra by the arm and the man closed the door. Alejandra was about to scream when the light turned on. The girl held her index finger to her lips, while heavy footsteps sounded in the corridor she'd just left.

The man whispered in her ear. "Hurry, we don't have much time."

Alejandra nodded and recovered her travel documents bag. She looked at them as if asking, *and now what?*

As if on cue, he grinned and opened a second door that led to a grey corridor, which took them to the service parking lot.

As soon as they set foot outside, the girl pressed the open button on her car key and pushed Alejandra into the back seat.

"Keep down," she hushed.

Alejandra nodded and hid.

In the rear-view mirror, she watched the guy while he threw the garbage bag into a bin, returned the dolly load to its place by the entrance, closed the service door with a key and joined them in the car.

They drove in silence for a while, until the girl turned and looked at Alejandra who was more confused than scared.

"Hi, my name is Sam, and this is Greg. You can sit normally now."

"I'm Alejandra."

"We know," the girl said and extended her a flyer.

It read: "First-time gang rape for sweet Alex. She thinks she is coming to dance the tango on Broadway, but she's up for a small surprise…"

The flyer had the same photo Pablo had seen, with Fermin's hand up her parts.

Realization fell over her like a ton of bricks. Could this be? Could Fermin had set everything up?

"How could I've been so stupid?" she bobbed her head in disbelief, tears streaming down her face.

"Hey girl, don't cry… those things happen, you know?"

"What were you doing in the closet?" she managed to ask after crying some more.

"Essentially: waiting for you," the guy said.

"Greg, stop it!" the girl admonished when she noticed Alejandra's scared face. "Ok, here is the tale… We don't clean here regularly. Just came today to replace a guy from work. He said there was funky stuff going on in here, and we like funky stuff *a lot*. He called in sick today to the other job, so we offered to cover for him. Extra money is always good, you know? First, we found the travel bag in the cleaning closet and that caught our attention, then we overheard that Vermin-guy, bragging and talking about tonight, and then saw you rehearsing… Gosh! *You are so good.* When we found the flyer, well, it was a bit too funky for our liking, so we decided to stay a bit later, just in case you needed a ride. I mean… we don't want you to think that all Americans are psychopaths. Most people are decent around here…"

"You guys saved my life…"

"Yeah, well… heroes for a day. One more thing crossed out from our bucket list," Greg chimed in and grinned.

Alejandra chuckled.

"Is there a cheap hotel in a safe area you can drop me by?"

"Yeah, about that… we have a place with two bedrooms and use only one. We're looking for a roommate. You can stay for the night and tomorrow decide what to do."

"Really?"

"Yeah," the guy said, again, looking at her in the rear mirror.

"Thanks," Alejandra murmured, blushing.

His eyes were intense enough to speak volumes about his intentions, but he didn't look like a rapist, and they had saved her from a very ugly fate. Alejandra's hand went to touch the young Virgin Mary pendant hanging from her neck, thanking her for this miracle, and also asking for protection from whatever came next.

Chapter 5

Rob found his friend already sitting at his favorite table by the window and playing distractedly with a jewelry box, oblivious of the manicured lawn of the golf course and the players walking by. At another table by a wall, two of his bodyguards watched everything with hawk eyes.

Rob nodded and they nodded back.

"What did you order?" he asked, pulling a chair and sitting smoothly.

"Just assorted Spanish tapas and Ventus. Have you heard of that wine?" Hack said.

"Nice little vineyard from Argentina. Good choice."

"Glad you approve." Hack nodded shortly and trained his piercing blue eyes on him. "So what was the rush about? Something about the results?"

"No, man. Your health is picture-perfect. You're ready for an Ironman competition, or to get married..."

Hack chuckled and shook his head a couple of times. "So, what is it?"

"I need a big favor." Rob pulled his favorite puppy face, complete with a pout and big glossy eyes.

"Anything but money." Hack's lips curled in a lopsided smirk.

"Man, you're killing me. The money isn't for me, it's for opening a small clinic of my own. I've got to get out of that place."

A shiver shook Rob's shoulders, his expression spooked.

His friend didn't flinch.

They had been like brothers since toddlerhood, and Hack knew all his tricks. Rob loved and hated it. Hack was just trying to save him from himself, but this time it was different. *Isn't it always?*

"Rob, you know I won't lend you the money. Now, tell me the tale. Maybe I can help you find another way out."

"Alright." A deep sigh escaped from his chest, again. "I received an ultimatum from Roger Leven, the clinic's vice-president. If I don't follow the standard procedures, they'll kick me out, sue *me* and *my father* for a hundred million bucks and make sure I lose my license."

Hack whistled.

"What happened? Did you send more people to Dr. Quack?"

Dr. Quack was the pet name they gave to Hack's functional medicine doctor. It had been Rob's recommendation. The man was a miracle worker.

"Worse... I'm *becoming* Dr. Quack." His lips twitched to one side into something between a pout and a smirk. "Following Roger's advice, I started reading the literature and discovered something pretty interesting: many drugs are substances isolated from plants. When you use the original source the side effects are always constructive, while in the case of drugs, they are always destructive."

"Meaning, switching to the real thing resolves multiple problems at the same time..." Hack chimed in.

"It gets even worse. Emboldened by these findings, I enrolled in the functional medicine certification course and the information there is mind-blowing. Just implementing lifestyle changes increase health markers threefold, reducing recurring business drastically. It's costing the clinic a small fortune... I've become a liability."

"Shit, that's a misaligned business model. Did you ask your father for help?"

"Well, the problem is that he's building a clinic for them. So Roger threatened him too to the point that my father is considering disinheriting me to save the company. He did offer a deal, but I can't accept his conditions."

"Which are?"

"I have to marry Millicent Pearson."

If he were a cartoon, Hack's eyes would have popped out of their sockets. "You can't do that!"

"Don't worry, I don't plan to." Rob shook his head emphatically.

"Didn't he give you any alternative options?"

"Not really."

"Doesn't he know she's a crazy bitch?" Hack insisted, a hint of desperation in his voice.

"I'm not sure. Problem is, he saw a picture of me in a demonstration, leathered up. Now he thinks I've become gay—as if that was possible—and could use some *tough love to walk straight again*." His fingers quoted the last part in the air.

Hack snorted.

"Not funny, man..." Rob chuckled. "Well, ok, it *is* funny."

"Why don't you ask any of your partners to marry you?"

Rob shook his head, serious now. "None of them are *suitable*. You know I prefer my girls submissive. There's no better high than when they enter *the zone* and become putty in your hands. Problem is, most submissives are also masochists. They enjoy suffering. It's one thing to play with them in a safe environment, and another one is to wake up by them in the morning. The ideal would be someone who is malleable in the bedroom and strong outside. I'm not sure that woman even exists, or if she would be interested in me."

"Can't you fund a clinic on your own? Get a loan from the bank?"

Rob snorted. "Not even the mob would lend me money. My father made sure of that."

Hack pulled the top of his short hair and let it slide between his fingers. "How long has this mess been rolling?"

"Four months ago I showed Roger the clinical studies displaying better results for my functional medicine patients compared with the regular ones. Two days later, I received the first notice from the legal department. After a week, my father invited me to fish with him, just to give me an ultimatum. Since then, I've been living a double life: telling my patients to buy the medicines but use the other protocols instead. They'll catch me sooner or later, and I'll probably lose my license and end up in jail, but... I just can't keep using only prescriptions when there are better options. My patients have put *their lives* in *my hands*. They trust me. I just can't deceive them. I'd rather give up medicine altogether."

Hack was lost in thought for five long minutes. Rob knew that face all too well. He was processing information and assessing possibilities. He finally made a tsk sound and focused again on his friend.

"Well, maybe you should get married. Not to Millicent, but someone else who fits the role. I'm doing much better with Janice in my life."

"She's a sweetheart." Rob smiled and the outer corners of his eyes crinkled. "So, how did it go?"

"What?"

"Did you propose?"

"Oh, that. Yeah..."

"And?"

"Man, gossip is for women, haven't you heard?"

Rob snickered. "Of course it is. Women gossip, men share news. Now, share. How did it go?"

Hack rolled his eyes. "She accepted the ring, only after I admitted it had a GPS in it."

"Oh shit..."

Hack waved his hand dismissively. "But... she doesn't want to marry me."

"Why the hell not?"

"That's exactly what I asked. She says she doesn't believe in the vows of marriage, that nobody can honestly assure another person that will love them for the rest of their lives. And you know how she is about keeping her word…"

"Mmm, she thinks too much…"

"That's what I said. It didn't go well…"

Chapter 6

Alejandra

Alejandra applied the last layer of mascara and looked at herself in the mirror. She was looking darn hot. Red lips, dark makeup over porcelain skin, and of course, black eyeliner encasing her beautiful brown eyes. Her crazy curly hair was straight for the night, and she had combed it to one side.

Today, it was four months since she'd arrived in New York; four months since she'd last danced, and a month since she officially became illegal in the country. She desperately needed a reminder of who she really was. Not only had her name changed, working with the cleaning crew was crawling slowly under her skin, and she was starting to lose her identity in the daily maelstrom.

The first day with Greg and Sam, Alejandra had called her parents but didn't tell them the whole truth. She'd told them things didn't go well, but that she was safe and looking for another gig. The return plane ticket was with Fermin—Vermin as Sam called him—and she didn't have the money to buy another one. Her father told her to use his credit card, but she decided to be an adult for once, to stay and work, and buy a ticket on her own. Maybe, just maybe, she could even get a tiny part dancing somewhere so she could show her parents she wasn't a total loser.

But as time rushed her along, she felt she was losing pieces of herself. Greg and Sam were pressing her to become a trio, and it wasn't for her, but the flesh is weak and if she didn't get a partner, sooner or later she would give in.

One, be nice. Two, do the job.

Those had been the basic rules of her job in the cleaning crew. They were simple but not negotiable. They had been very challenging for Alejandra who was essentially a free spirit. She'd resorted to creating a character, Alex, and impersonating it, calling in her short but efficient theater studies. It was *sliding in the zone* in a different way. That character was spineless and could easily accept a trio to avoid conflict if Greg pressed her enough.

She needed to be herself again, at least for a night, and her own self was not nice. She was kind but not nice. So today, she was going to dance the tango.

Alejandra checked her clothes in the mirror. Her little black dress was long to her knees but open on the side. It paired perfectly with her leather stiletto shoes.

"Someone's getting laid tonight..." Samantha gave a catcall from the door.

"Sure. You are." Alejandra chuckled.

"C'mon, Alex, I told you more than once that you can join us, Greg would love to have you..."

"Thanks, Sam. Appreciate it, but threesomes are not really my thing."

"And what is your thing? I haven't seen you with anyone."

Alejandra turned around and looked at her. "Maybe I'm the last romantic. I still believe in love."

"Hum. Good luck with that..." the girl said, twisting her lips comically. "So, where are you going?"

"I heard at work that tonight is tango night at Club Passion. I haven't gone out...ever, so I thought it would be fun."

"It does sound like fun."

"Would you guys like to come? I can teach you some moves."

"Alright. Let's do it," Greg chimed in, poking his head through the side of the door.

Alejandra rolled her eyes.

* * *

The club was bubbling. One of the floors played tango, but there were others with meringue, reggaeton and Latin-mix rhythms.

When they arrived at the dance floor, the song *La Cumparsita* was playing and Alejandra smirked at the sight of people walking back and forth.

"So," Greg spoke in her ear. She looked at Sam, and the other girl nodded, grinning. Alejandra didn't understand how she could be so eager to see her man with another woman. No matter how much she tried, she just couldn't.

"It's like this. Give me your hand." She placed it on her waist. "Now we hold the other like this."

Greg extended his arm and she pulled it back, forming an arch. "Ready? Now you walk two steps forward and one to the side, get it?"

He followed her instructions, and they managed to get the basic steps in place. He was wooden but enthusiastic.

They danced one soundtrack and she noticed he was starting to get the hang of it.

"You are doing it very well, congrats!" she yelled over the music.

"Really?" His big puppy eyes glowed.

"Yes," she grinned and nodded a few times.

His eyes squinted and he grinned back. He lowered his head to the side to talk in her ear.

"And when do I get to grab your bum and have your pussy on my leg?" he asked, nuzzling her earlobe.

"Never!" she answered emphatically, wriggling out of the embrace.

He sighed.

"Why are you such a stuck-up bitch?"

Alejandra thought of many ways to answer, but she chose her preferred line. "What can I say? I'm *porteña.*" She stuck her chin out defiantly.

"You're not being nice…"

"You are not being nice either. Besides… I don't need to be nice. We are not at work now. This is *me.*" She turned around and left him there.

She knew he was smiling. Greg was such a horndog.

Without even trying, she'd adopted the tango way of walking, where the front leg starts straight and then bends while the back leg stays straight, creating a beautiful pace and expressing a cocky attitude. Many eyes on the floor followed her now as she made her way to the bar.

She hadn't walked far when a hand closed over her arm; warm, with long fingers. Her body reacted to his touch.

"Dance with me," someone whispered in her ear. She turned to see the strong, square chin of a guy. Looking up, she found two mesmerizing hazel green eyes, boring into hers, framed by short ruffled dark blond hair. He was tanned and looked like a surfer in expensive clothes. Yet his eyes were deep, beautiful, and demanding.

There was something hypnotic about this man, something that contradicted his appearance, but was very real. Her head nodded and she put one hand on his shoulder.

He didn't waste time. His open palm pushed her back until their chests touched. The other hand held hers and he pressed their faces cheek over cheek softly. *El Choclo* was playing now. The first step marked the dance, he put his knee right between her legs, and up to her *need.*

Alejandra fell easily in the hands of this skilled dancer. Tango is all about the man, and his ability to lead, and the woman and her ability to surrender. She'd only danced with Fermin for the last three years, and before him, there had only been older men, too old for her to even consider away from the dance floor. This man's touch was completely different. It was fluid and involving and caring. He managed to bring the dancer and the woman together.

The music sank in her bones and her feet flew. He guided her smoothly, his intent clear through the touch of his chest and his hands. It was as if he was trying to see how much more he could make her do, how putty-like she was in his hands. Her feet drew the arabesques of tango on the dancefloor. Eights, and scissors, and breaks, in a succession that made other couples stop and watch. This song had two tempos; the first half was reasonably slow, while the second half was crazy fast. As she let loose, she showed more of herself, until the point when she lifted her leg and placed her foot on his shoulder. He seemed surprised for a second, then a grin opened up on his face, as if he had received a Christmas present, and his eyes bored into hers with an intensity that melted her to the core. From there, their dance went from hot saloon-tango to pure performance. When the music ended, she had both her legs around his waist and her torso backwards, resting on his bent thigh.

People broke into applause, and she felt truly happy for the first time in a long, long time.

Another song started, it was *Por una Cabeza*, but she noticed they were not dancing. Actually, he had picked her up and was walking toward the far end of the club, with her legs still around his waist, and his hand firm on her bottom. She knew she should stop him, but she couldn't find the strength to come out of the daze. It felt too good.

He went to a shadowy corner. The bar curved all the way there, but the bartender was on the other side about ten feet away. There were no people around.

"What…" she started asking.

"Shh. Feel the music," he said.

She sighed and closed her eyes.

He turned her around and placed himself at her back, moved her hair sideways and nuzzled her neck. They were protected by the bar and the darkness and the music. Only their upper torsos were dimly visible.

Her head fell back, and he inhaled.

"You smell so good," he murmured in her ear.

His hands moved on her body, one hugging her tightly, while the other trailed south slowly.

"We can't," she breathed, catching his roaming hand to stop him. What was it with this man? Or was her need so strong?

Fermin was an amazing dancer, yet she only felt rejection for him as a man. Pablo had been her lover for six years, and she would never let him become too close in public. It just wasn't right. With this man... she was in his hands.

"I can't leave you like this. Let me finish what we started." His voice was soothing.

She felt cared for, cherished, *loved*?

"I can't have sex with you. We're not a couple. I don't even know you," she spoke softly, fully aware that whatever happened at this time was his call. She was too out of it to resist him. She actually didn't want to resist him. Only the thought of being like this in public gave her pause.

"Nobody will notice," he purred.

"No?" she asked, but then his hand moved under her panties and all thoughts ceased.

He whispered in her ear and her body responded directly, bypassing her conscious mind. She could feel the sound embracing her, cuddling her, soothing her. "Listen to my voice. You're so exquisite, so beautiful. Put your head on my shoulder and relax every muscle. Yes, like this. You can trust me, I'll hold you. Feel me, feel how I pleasure you. You're so wet for me now. Yes, like this. Feel me, but don't move."

Her body was on fire, and his instruction not to move made it worse. She couldn't do anything but feel. It was like dancing the tango in a different way. He led, she surrendered. *Garganta con Arena* played now; it was a very emotional song that always made her cry.

"I can't take it anymore," she breathed, tears streaming down her face.

"What do you want?" he breathed.

"I want..."

"Do you want to come for me?"

"Yes…"

"Yes, please?"

"Yes, please…"

He turned her head and kissed her deeply, hungrily, while his fingers danced hard and fast. She convulsed and came violently, waves of pleasure traveling from her core up her belly button and down her toes.

Her legs buckled and he held her effortlessly, guiding her to a seat. She felt deeply cared for. Sated and happy, she relaxed into his embrace.

Alejandra came out of daze slowly. He'd called the bartender and had a glass in front of her.

"Here, drink." It was water with lime. Cold, fresh and just what she needed to wake up and realize what had happened.

"Oh my gosh," she said, moving away from him. "What have I done?"

He smiled. "It was just a thank you gift for a beautiful dance."

He patted the booth at his side and Alejandra sat before even thinking. She took a deep breath and sipped her water.

"I've never done anything like this," she whispered into her drink.

"I know…"

She looked into his eyes to see if he really believed her. And yes, he understood, probably more than herself.

"You could have fucked me, and you didn't…"

"Don't I know it," he sighed theatrically and looked at his bulge. She followed his eyes and realized that his pants seemed about to explode. He was big. Her eyes opened wide and went back to watching his.

"Why didn't you?"

"Do you want me to? We still can…"

"No."

He sighed.

"It wouldn't have been a thank-you-gift, it would've been taking advantage of you."

She blinked several times to clear her tears, many conflicting emotions coursing through her.

He seemed to notice and caressed her face. "Look. I know you're not comfortable with what happened, but you were in *the zone*, and everyone noticed you on the dance floor. I have to go now, and leaving you like this was dangerous." He looked at her very serious now. "Gorgeous, I respect your choice to not have sex, but others won't. Every man in the club could sense your need. It's been how long? Six months?"

She inhaled sharply, surprised. "How do you know?"

He smirked. "I'm a doctor."

"Yeah, right." She waved her hand.

He chuckled.

"What's your name?"

"Alex."

"Pleased to meet you, Alex. I'm Rob."

He extended his palm and they shook hands.

She giggled.

"I'm going to do something I never ever do, give you my cell number." Rob took a card from his back pocket. "If you ever need a friend, if you ever want to talk, if you ever want to dance with me again, just call."

She took the card. "Thanks."

"I know you're about to throw it in the first garbage can you find. Don't. Keep it."

"What are you, psychic?"

"Nope. I'm a doctor." He grinned.

"Yeah, right." She rolled her eyes.

Chapter 7

Rob

Rob sat at the wheel of his Aston Martin Vanquish, adjusted his still-stiff package and smelled his fingers. That had been a hot woman. Sweet Alex, so intense, so submissive. What was a professional tango dancer doing in a club like this? Club Passion mostly attracted people from the Caribbean. He liked the colors, and the accents and the passion. It was like being a tourist without leaving New York.

He'd hoped to see some Argentineans tonight. They were usually very good at hiding and not calling attention to themselves in normal settings, but he'd never dreamed of finding a real rose of Buenos Aires, dancing the tango as only they could.

After smelling his fingers once again, he turned on the ignition to head home. The engine purred and he chuckled.

"Don't be jealous. You'll always be my favorite." He patted the steering wheel and pressed the accelerator pedal. The engine roared. "That's how you like it, don't you, girl?"

His condo was over the Hudson River, in Battery Park City. He had some very neat views from his living room of the water and the Statue of Liberty. Of course, it was not his, but his father's. He was graciously allowed to live there—for now.

While crossing the bridge to Manhattan, his mind came back to his most pressing issues. Could he find a wife who met the conditions his father required and try to make a deal? He quickly added some of his own. She definitely needed to know how to dance the tango, and she had to have amazing, flexible legs, and red lips and brown eyes with thick eyelashes… *Oh man, you're infatuated already.*

The tires screeched on the pavement when he took West Street going south at forty miles per hour.

He pressed the brake pedal to slow down, but the car didn't stop. In fact, it accelerated.

Shit.

In a split-second decision, his right hand unlocked his seatbelt and his left one opened the door. His torso steered, propelling him out of the vehicle. Falling on the pavement was rough but didn't hurt as much as he expected. *Give it time.*

His eyes followed in dismay while his favorite girl ran like a minion of hell and hit a tree, exploding.

Rob caught his breath when he saw some of the flying pieces coming toward him. *No, no.* The noise was shattering when they fell all around him, but none hit him.

Thank you, Lord. Thank you, angels. Thank you whoever you are!

Only once the immediate danger was over, did he take the time to examine himself. He'd saved his life by a miracle, but not without injury. One of his legs bent at a weird angle, and one of his arms didn't respond. All in all, it had been a cheap price to pay. If he'd been drinking tonight instead of dancing with Alex, he wouldn't be here.

His still usable hand pulled his phone and speed-dialed Hack's number, right before the pain took over.

* * *

Alex

Alex climbed to the back seat of Greg's car and hid herself behind the small screen of her cellphone. Greg managed several crews that worked the night shift cleaning cinemas, and they were just finishing for the day. Her feet hurt, her back hurt and her arms hurt, but she knew better than to complain. Greg was driving them home, with Sam by his side. They'd both been very upset with her since the night at the club. She'd been playing Miss Prim for the last four months just to fuck a total stranger in public. They were right, of course.

Alejandra couldn't understand them. It was as if for them sex was just a fun game. I tickle you here, you tickle me there and we all have a great time. It wasn't like that for her. Not at all. For her, sex was part of something bigger and deeper. Intimacy. Love. Trust. Eventually children. And the hinted promise of growing old together. Of course, she didn't have much evidence for her claim after what happened. Sadly enough, because of the way she was wired, since that night, this guy was not just a guy, not for her anyway.

And this was a problem.

Greg was her boss and had his head on the chopping block for hiring her under wraps. He did take a cut of her salary to compensate for the taxes, and she paid half of the rent when they were living together in the apartment. Yet… she was thankful she had a decent job, food on the table and a roof over her head. A bit more and she would be able to buy a ticket back home. *And this horrible nightmare will end.*

She tried to read the local news to put aside her thoughts and the aggressive vibe coming from the front of the car. Right there in bold letters, it described a car accident.

Dr. Robert MacArthur, son of construction magnate Joseph MacArthur, had an accident in the early morning. The car exploded after hitting a tree at eighty miles per hour.
The police are investigating the case and can't provide details yet.
Dr. MacArthur suffered a mild concussion, and one broken arm and leg, according to the medical report.

"Oh my gosh," Alex exclaimed.

"What happened?" Sam asked over her shoulder.

Alejandra handed her the phone without saying a word. On the cover, there was a picture of Rob and the name was the one on the card. It had to be the same guy.

"Shit, this must have been right after leaving the club," Sam commented.

Alex nodded, her eyes far in the distance. She noticed that Greg was looking at her in the mirror, but she was too bewildered to hide her feelings.

"You really fell for that guy, didn't you?"

Alejandra lifted and bent her legs, hugging them; then put her forehead on the knees to hide her tears.

After lunch, she took the card and studied every detail for the tenth time. The black paper was thick and glossy, and the letters, written in gold, very delicate. It just had a name and cell phone number. It was a personal card, not a business one.

"I don't want anything from him. I just want to hear his voice and know he is ok. That's all," she muttered her speech as if rehearsed.

She nodded one time, took a deep breath and called the number on the card.

"Who's this?" Rob answered. The sound was weak and reluctant.

"Alejandra, I mean, Alex," her voice so low it would be a miracle if he heard.

"Alex? What a lovely surprise!"

"I saw the news and wanted to make sure you were alright."

"Oh that… and I thought that you wanted to dance with me again. Maybe you want to do something else," he teased.

Alejandra chuckled. "As long as you don't invite me for a ride. Man, you are a reckless driver…"

"Actually I'm not," he clipped sharply, taking her by surprise. "Listen," he added in a lighter tone, "would you like to come and visit me? I'm at the hospital and bored to death. It would make my day to see your sweet face while I suffer."

"I-I can't," she stammered. "I just wanted to see if you were ok…"

"But you can't *see* if I'm ok on the phone. C'mon, just a little visit. Promise I won't touch you. I have a broken leg and arm. There isn't really much I can do."

After three eternally long seconds, Alejandra sighed. "Alright, but just a couple of hours. Give me the address."

* * *

Rob

The girl entering the room only slightly resembled the femme fatale he'd danced with. She looked like her younger sister. Poodle curly hair and almost no makeup, just a touch of black eyeliner and pink lip gloss gave her face a teenage look.

She had faded jeans and a dark blue high neck tank top. Both her boots and jacket were made out of real leather. The lady had a thing for classic, it seemed.

"Hi," she said shyly, tucking her hair behind her ear.

"Hi, gorgeous. Thanks for coming." Rob turned on the charm.

Alex sat on a chair by his side. "How are you feeling?"

"As if I jumped from a moving car." He chuckled, making her smile.

He extended his healthy hand to her and she placed hers on top of it. Rob felt a pang of something hard to define. He had a family and friends, and enough lovers to make most men jealous, yet, he would be completely alone if not for this girl, and completely devoid of human contact if it were not for her hand.

The door opened and a nurse entered, clicking on the floor with her heels. She was in her thirties, with bleached hair, too much makeup and too much cleavage exposed. He knew her kind all too well. Ninety-nine percent of nurses were dedicated, hard-working, kind and re-sourceful. The best people he knew were among them. But in each hospital, there was one of these.

"Dr. MacArthur, here is your painkiller." She put a small plastic re-ceptacle with two pills on the side table, bending down and trying to show off her fake boobs.

"Thanks, Becky. You're a ray of sunshine. What would I do without you?"

The woman beamed at his flirtatious charm.

Her smile fell when she saw Alex and Rob holding hands.

"I'm sorry, miss. I'll have to ask you to leave. Only close family members can be here out of the visitation hours."

Alex was about to retrieve her hand, but Rob gripped it tighter.

"You didn't see her before, did you? This is Alex, my fiancé."

"Oh, I'm sorry. I didn't know you had a fiancé."

"Now you do." He grinned, showing miles of teeth, and fully aware of the blow he'd just given her. It was petty, he knew, but he still enjoyed it thoroughly. Rob was not gold digger material, but he looked the part, so he'd met plenty of these before. He'd also seen how their demeanor changed when they found out he was permanently and hopelessly broke.

The woman left the room with a scowl on her face and her back bent.

"So," he said to a bewildered Alex, "tell me about your job."

Chapter 8

Rob

With nothing else to do, Rob's mind worked all afternoon. Alex was sleeping, sitting on a chair with her head resting on her arms, and he'd taken his time to feel and comb her hair meantime. It was soft and smelled faintly of roses and something else. He could get used to seeing it on his pillow.

She hadn't talked much about how she arrived in the U.S. or why, and Rob felt it was still an open wound, so he didn't ask. All he gathered was that it had been a mistake, she worked in a cleaning crew, and soon would be able to buy a ticket back home. What was most remarkable about this little fact was that she had managed to save money earning less than minimum wage. How did she do it? And more importantly, would she be able to do the same for him? If he could convince his father that she would, then the old man might give him the clinic. *A man can only hope.*

The door opened and a very upset Joe MacArthur entered the room, his big frame dominating the space and making everything feel obnoxiously small. He'd traveled all the way from the Emirates and come right from the airport. The wheeled suitcase held in his right hand was a mute token of paternal sacrifice toward the yet to be prodigal son. There were bags under his eyes, and a worry mark cut his forehead right in the middle.

Rob felt sorry for the old man. It was not an easy task to have him as family. He crossed his lips with his index finger, cutting the tirade his father had prepared.

The man looked at Alex sleeping, and his expression changed, softening. "Who's this?"

"My fiancé." Rob smiled.

"How much did she cost?"

Rob's smile vanished, his eyes became stormy. "Father, do not insult my girl," he growled, surprising his father and himself alike.

"What is a pretty thing like her doing with a fag like you?" the old man asked, after assessing her profile.

"Lots of things, but gentlemen kiss and don't tell." Rob was smiling again, but it didn't reach his eyes. If only he didn't need the money...

The old man exhaled noisily and took a seat. Rob noticed that Alex was awake; her breathing was not deep and regular anymore. He put the back of his hand on her cheek. She relaxed and played along. Rob loved her ability to understand what he wanted. It had shown while dancing, but it apparently didn't end there.

"Let's get this straight. Are you a fag or not?"

"What if I were? Are you judging people for what they do behind closed doors?"

"You were not behind closed doors in those pictures. Are you or not?" the man repeated, the vein of his neck showing.

"No," Rob answered flatly.

His father sighed.

Joe MacArthur was old school, a funny way to say homophobic. Not in the sense of discriminating against others. He just didn't want *it* in his family.

"Are you a junkie then?"

"Of course not!"

"Then what were you doing?"

"In those pictures? I was giving a demonstration."

"I don't understand…" his father murmured to himself shaking his head and looking at the floor. His eyes zeroed on Rob again. "What happened with the car?"

"You wouldn't believe me if I told you…"

"Try me."

Rob sighed. "Alright. I entered West Street at 40 miles per hour, so I hit the brake to slow down. The car accelerated instead of stopping. I jumped. The speed kept growing and she hit a tree. Not sure how fast, but over sixty. Not only that, but the car also exploded."

"Are you saying what I think you are saying?"

"That somebody tried to kill me? Yes."

Joe MacArthur covered his face with his hands and squeezed the corners of his eyes, the index finger going to the outside and the middle finger to the inside.

Alex shook as if trying to get up, and Rob kept her in place, pressing her nape.

"Any guess of who could be? The guy from the cross in those photos?"

Rob chuckled.

"The only people who are upset with me at the moment are from the clinic. Hack's working on this. He'll find out what happened."

"And the cute gold digger?" Joe signaled Alex with his head.

Rob snorted. "No gold digger would want anything to do with me, and you know it. I'm surprised you managed to get Millicent on board, actually."

"It wasn't cheap, believe me," the old man grunted.

"I'm not marrying her. I'm marrying this little darling," Rob said, moving the hair away from her face.

Alex inhaled sharply and lifted her head, looking at Rob with eyes like saucers.

"Well, hello there. Glad you decided to join us."

"I was awake all along," she answered Rob's father in a low voice.

His smile grew bigger. "I know, sweetheart."

She blushed.

"So, are you marrying my son or is it one of his machinations?"

She looked at him, and then at Rob. He pleaded with her through his eyes and took her hand.

"We are thinking about it. Not a definite date yet," she answered with her eyes on the floor and her color rising even more.

The man crackled. "She's a horrible liar. I like that."

Rob chuckled and caressed her face.

"Truth is, I'll do my best to convince her. She meets your requirements… and mine," he added, smiling, and this time it did reach his eyes.

"Really? How come?" Genuine interest showed in the old man's hawk gaze.

"She arrived in the country four months ago from Argentina. She's earning minimum wage and has savings. Imagine what she can do with my modest income."

The old man shook his head.

"Not enough. She can be good with her own finances, but to keep you out of trouble you need a royal bitch, like Millicent. This little lady won't do. You will be running circles around her in no time and stealing her money. In two months she'll be emotionally and financially broke, trying to start over."

Alex looked at Rob with worried eyes, and it just broke his heart. Why did his father have to do this every time? Put everyone against him? *I'm not the spoiled narcissistic piece of work he sees in me, am I?*

She seemed to collect herself and studied his father levelly.

"Thanks for letting me know, *sir*. I will keep it in mind. But let me tell you something: with a horrible father like you, it's no wonder that Rob has issues. It would be a miracle if he didn't."

She stood up fast, not giving Rob time to secure her hand.

"I have to go to work now." She kissed his forehead. "I'll come back tomorrow."

"I'll be waiting."

She nodded one time to Rob's father and left the room with her chin up, walking with a tango pace.

Both men watched her go with smiles plastered on their faces.

After she left the room, Joe MacArthur whistled. "She's a keeper."

"And you haven't seen her dance yet... So, are you helping me with the clinic?"

His father shook his head, collecting his thoughts. "Let's do something. You're going to be out of work for a couple of months. I'll pay you ten grand a month for six months. If you manage to end the period with five grand plus the girl's money untouched, and you marry her, then I give you space to have your clinic in the new office building I'm finishing downtown. But," the bushy eyebrows of the man rose, "you'll need to find a way to furnish it and buy the materials on your own."

"Dad!" Rob's voice took a whining high pitch, "how am I supposed to do that?"

"None of my business," the man answered, rising. "Your mother took the first flight from Calcutta when she found out what happened. She'll be here tonight. If you try to take advantage of her, I will not only not help you, but will also disinherit you, and take the apartment and what's left of the car. This was the last straw. Am I clear?"

"Do you really think I'm that hopeless?"

"Honestly... I used to, but considering how fast Hack moves his resources for you, and how this little kitten tried to scratch me, I'm starting to think there is probably something good in you I haven't seen yet... maybe because you were *too busy whining like a spoiled brat and asking for money.*"

* * *

"Hello, sweetheart," Anne MacArthur, Rob's mother, sang softly while closing the door behind her.

"Hey, Mom. You shouldn't have come all the way from India for a broken leg," Rob said, emotion rising.

"Did you have any doubt?" She smiled, her eyes filling with tears.

"No," Rob answered, his own eyes blurry as well.

She sat by him and took his healthy hand.

"What mischief did you get yourself into this time?" She asked, smiling.

"Honest to God, this time I was trying to do the right thing."

"Oh, that explains a lot…" She laughed and Rob joined her.

"It's good to see you. I missed you," he said.

"Oh, honey. I missed you too." She kissed his forehead and combed his hair away from his eyes. "Alright, so you became gay for a day and practiced witchcraft at the office, and now you're getting married to a cleaning lady who happens to be an illegal immigrant… did I miss something?"

Rob chuckled. "It sounds weird, doesn't it?"

"Just a little…" His mom grinned. "So, let's start from the beginning… what about this girl your father wants you to meet? He said you rejected her upfront."

Rob sighed, still smiling. "Do you remember that business training Hack's father put us through? The one about knowing the inner limits and power?"

"The one where you had to walk over hot coals?"

"No. The next one."

"Oh, the one in that bizarre house in the middle of nowhere…"

"Exactly. That one was about BDSM."

"Oh, goodness… that was the last one you attended. Decided to study medicine instead of working with your father after it…"

"Exactly."

"What happened?"

"Millicent Pearson handcuffed me and stepped on my throat with her five-inch heels. If not for Hack, I would be dead."

"She's a psychopath?"

"I don't know. She's a crazy bitch for sure…"

"What did you do to her that made her this mad?"

Rob arched an eyebrow. "Blaming the victim?"

"No, looking for the trigger," her mother answered with mischief.

"I gave her an orgasm. She took it as an insult."

Anne's mouth rounded in a silent *Oh*... "And that's the woman your father wanted you to marry."

"Exactly..."

She nodded one time. "I understand your marital choices now."

"No, you don't. Alex is a truly remarkable woman."

She patted his arm softly. "I believe you. You have an eye for hidden gems. So, the gay part?"

"Does it matter to you?" Rob was starting to get tired of the interrogation.

"I'm curious."

He sighed. "Well, in that course I discovered I was a natural dom, and particularly good at it. Do you really want to hear more details?"

His mother's eyes shone with mischief. "Honey, here's my own little secret: I'm not a virgin. Shocking, I know..."

Rob chuckled. "Alright. It seems I'm able to make both men and women—and everything in between—arrive at orgasm following their inner paths of stimulation, once they gave explicit consent of course, even if they are unorthodox or had never been explored before. If you saw the images, you probably noticed I never actually touched the guy. I led him only with a whip. And he was straight as well."

"Why did you do it?" Anne let her confusion show.

"I was invited to talk in a private panel about hedonism. The event had many speakers. It revolved around the sexual spectrum and identity diversity. Some were trying to show it was not natural, but a construct. Some said it was biological, but the result of food, water and electromagnetic pollution. Others said it was just a natural social evolution and we needed to rethink society under these diverse family structures. My main point was that we shouldn't confuse sexual pleasure with love or sexual inclination. I was explaining how orgasm is a physical release that can be attained by physical stimulation only, and this guy dared me into a demonstration. He was shocked, but a good enough sport afterwards."

"What was the conclusion of the event?"

"I don't know if there was one. As far as I'm concerned, natural or not, to each their own. An attorney made an interesting point when it comes to legislation: private should be private. The government has no business there. And the first amendment should never be violated like it was in Canada."

Satisfied with the explanation, Anne changed the subject:

"And the witchcraft?"

Rob huffed playfully.

"It's called functional medicine. I took a certification program."

"And?" she encouraged.

"It's plain medicine, but dives into the research and uses what works instead of only artificial, patented products."

This definitely called her attention.

"Example?"

Rob moved his healthy arm vaguely.

"It's a holistic method that takes the human body as an ecosystem. It uses chemicals when needed, but also plants and lifestyle changes when possible. And more importantly: it goes right to the research."

Anne grinned enthusiastically. "That's exciting. Grandma meets science?"

Rob nodded. "It's a little bit more complicated than that, but you could say so."

His mother was thoughtful for a minute, assessing the information.

"So you really were doing things right…" she said softly.

"I told you so!" Rob exclaimed.

Anne chuckled and opened her purse.

"Look what I brought you, for your collection."

She showed him a package that contained a copper bowl with hand-carved designs. She placed it on the small side table and hit it with a wooden striker. The sound was rich and powerful, reverberating in the middle of his chest.

"This is a Tibetan singing bowl. It's very ancient and holds many secrets. When I saw it, it just called your name. They say it can aid healing."

"I'm speechless…" Rob was looking at the present in awe.

Chapter 9

Alejandra

Alejandra arrived at the hospital feeling uneasy. She was tired after two days without proper sleep. Greg had given her the nastiest jobs, and her attraction for Rob seemed unhealthy. She was so close to having her ticket home, yet she was risking it all, and for what? A guy she didn't even know? Granted, Pablo had never managed to give her an orgasm as powerful as the one of the club, but pleasure came in a fine wine bottle turned into a Molotov bomb. Dangerous stuff. Decadent, in more than one sense, stuff...

When Alex passed the nurses' station on Rob's floor, a hand snaked and grabbed her arm rudely.

"You can't come in," the fake blond of the day before told her, venom pouring down her invisible fangs.

"But..."

"Dr. MacArthur is with his *real* fiancé. He asked me to stop you, so she doesn't see you." The woman folded her arms and smirked while the information sank in.

Alejandra closed her eyes to half-mast and took her phone.

"Hey there," Rob's voice smiled at her.

"I'm on your floor, but that bleached bitch, Becky, says you ordered her to stop me. Something about you being with your real fiancé..."

He inhaled sharply. "And you believe her?"

"No, or I wouldn't be calling you."

"Good." He sighed. "Give the phone to her, please…" he said, his tone flat.

The nurse took the phone reluctantly and heard what Rob had to say. Her eyes went round, and she gave it back to Alejandra.

"Ha," the young woman said, lifting her chin and walking past the nurse. She didn't know what he said, nor did she care. "Y mañana cuando seas, descolado mueble viejo…" she sang softly the tune of *Cuesta abajo*, a classic, while her boots clicked on the floor.

When Alex approached Rob's bedroom, she could hear high pitched screams coming from inside.

"How can you insult me like this? I *will not* tolerate it," a woman screeched at the top of her lungs.

"Good, don't tolerate it and leave me alone," Rob answered loud enough to be heard.

"You traded me for what? A frigging maid?"

"I'm not trading you for her. You and I have never been a couple."

"We fucked and I have a ring, see? We are a couple."

"I didn't give you that ring, and about the night together… I still have nightmares about it."

Alejandra could feel the uneasiness in his voice. It wasn't a joke. The door opened violently to show a very tall woman. She was blond with grey eyes and slim like a broomstick. Her clothes were a Fifth Avenue ensemble and Alejandra didn't need to see to know her shoes had a red underside. Everything about her exuded power, money and arrogance.

"Leave and don't come back. Rob doesn't need a maid now," she said between clenched teeth, her eyes spitting fire.

Alejandra lifted her chin and looked at the woman nonchalantly. "Let him tell me," she said and moved fast under the woman's arm and into the bedroom.

The woman grabbed her by the hair.

"Don't touch her," Rob's voice came out strong and clear, with an authority Alejandra hadn't felt since the night they danced.

"I refuse to stay in the same room with her." The woman rebutted.

"There it's the door. You're free to leave." Rob's eyes were cold and dark, his voice, controlled.

"This is not the end of this conversation. The families made an arrangement, and you will have to oblige."

She left swinging her bony hips and avoiding looking at Alejandra.

"Millicent, I presume?" Alex asked, nonchalant.

"In the anorexic flesh," Rob sighed and fell back. "Could you help me here?"

"Sure." She approached him and organized his pillows so he would be comfortable.

"Thanks, you're a God-sent miracle," he murmured in her ear. Taking the back of her head with his healthy hand, he gave her a peck on her lips.

Alejandra smiled.

Rob urged her to sit and took her hand.

He tilted his head, "You look tired."

"That's because I *am* tired. I haven't slept properly in two days, remember?" She hesitated for a second and went on to say, "Look, I like coming to visit and talking with you, but I will not be able to keep it up for long."

"I know. You need to sleep sometimes. In a real bed."

She nodded.

"Ok, marry me then. Problem solved." He grinned and small wrinkles appeared on the outer corners of his eyes.

"Oh boy…" She giggled. "What's the purpose anyway? Your father will not give you the money. I'm not bitchy enough." She made a face.

"I don't care. I want you." There was a hypnotic intensity in his stare.

Alejandra felt she would oblige to whatever he asked if he looked at her long enough. She closed her eyes to break the contact and took a deep breath.

"I'm not a toy to be possessed, Rob. I'm a woman."

"Oh… I'm fully aware of that," he teased.

"Stop it," she laughed and then sobered. "Look, I like you, but I don't think it will work."

He sighed.

"You really don't think much of me after meeting my father, do you?" His eyes were sad.

She considered her answer carefully. "It was a timely reminder that what happens on the dance floor should stay on the dance floor."

"Then why did you come today?" he pressed.

"Because I said I would."

He caressed the side of her face with the back of his fingers and she closed her eyes, enjoying the buzz his touch gave her.

He took a deep breath. "Alright, I have a business proposal for you."

She opened her eyes just to roll them. "Let's hear it."

"I need someone to be with me when I go home tomorrow. To make the bed, take care of the delivery, keep me company..."

"Don't you need a nurse? Someone that, you know, help you with... stuff..."

"Like going to the toilet or having a shower?"

Alejandra blushed. "Yeah."

"I can manage the toilet, and for baths, there will be a nurse coming daily to check on me. My mother already arranged it."

"You have nosey parents too?"

Rob chuckled. "Oh yeah. So, are you staying with me?"

Alejandra shook her head slowly.

"I don't think that's a good idea."

"I won't touch you if you don't want, not a finger, and I'll double your salary."

"There is more to the story than you are telling me, isn't it? I will consider it IF you tell me all of it."

Rob sighed. *Alright.* "You already heard most of it. I need my own clinic. My father agreed to help only if I married Millicent because I'm not good with money—and he thinks I'm gay—so he wants someone able to keep me *walking straight.*"

Alejandra was very confused. "Gay?"

"Just for the record, I'm not."

"I know. Why did your father think you could be?"

"Mmm, he saw pictures of me pleasuring another man."

"Hum?"

"I don't want to talk about it right now... So this is what I really have in mind: We marry, I give you a green card, you give me my clinic. My father will cover my expenses while I'm off work. He agreed to give me the clinic if at the end of six months I manage to keep five grand and your money intact. So you see? You're perfectly safe."

She listened to what he had to say, a knot in her heart tightening with each word. Her eyes became sadder and sadder and there were tears when he finished. She really liked the guy, but for him, she was only a ticket to his clinic.

"I can't marry you," she said softly.

"Why the hell not? Your life will be far better than it is now. You will have residency."

"Who told you I want to be a resident?" She sighed. "I couldn't care less, but that's not the reason."

"Tell me what it is."

"Call me a romantic, but I still believe in love..."

He looked pained as if he had received a blow.

She broke down and cried. Not only for this selfish bastard, but for the other selfish bastard, the one that wanted her to be at home so he wouldn't be troubled, and yet the third selfish son of the bitch, the one that sold her the rainbow only to sink her in the mud, completely alone and far away from everything she knew and loved.

And she cried for herself, for her stubbornness, for not wanting to ask for help from her family to buy the frigging ticket back. She didn't want to come home and see her brothers' *I-told-you-so* looks. Oh gosh, what would they say if they knew she'd escaped by a hair from a pornhub? That she worked on a cleaning crew? She, the little princess, the one that took ballet lessons and didn't do anything in the house because she was always busy playing the piano, had finally learned to clean toilets...

"I'm sorry," she said when she finished spilling her sadness over the hospital sheets. "Not all those tears were for you."

"I know," he murmured.

"I won't be coming anymore."

He nodded. "I know."

She got up and he took her arm. "One thing."

"What?"

"Keep my card. If you ever need anything, and I mean *anything*, you call me, and I'll be there for you."

"Thanks." She took a second to collect herself and the tears that threatened to come again, then she lifted her chin, rolled her shoulders back and left.

Chapter 10

Rob

The sliding doors of the hospital opened, and a gust of wind air took Alex by surprise. Her hair painted dynamic arabesques in the wind as she tightened her clothes about herself. Summer was coming to an end, and soon it would be cold. She wondered how it would be to live in a city covered in snow. Buenos Aires had cold and rainy winters, but it never snowed.

Crying had put her in a weird state of mind. She didn't have the heart to go back home after the hospital. She was feeling too shaken to face anyone. Apparently, the tango malady had infected her blood, as she was falling for a man who was incredibly hot, but unable to see beyond his own belly button. If only she had her piano, or a guitar, something...

She wandered about and ended in *Don't Tell Mama*, a piano bar that opened its doors at five o'clock, earlier than most. The show started later, so she had the piano to herself.

After warming up the fingers with *Für Elise,* she moved to the tune that was singing in the back of her head, *Malevaje*. It told the tale of a fighter who had changed his ways because of a woman. She wanted this from Rob, if he wanted to be her man, to straighten up because she was worth it. Only apparently, she wasn't...

She softly sang the tune:

No me has dejado ni el pucho en la oreja (You didn't even let the cigarette on the ear)
De aquel pasado malevo y feroz (From that past, outlaw and fierce,)
Ya know me falta pa completar (I only need to complete)
Más que ir a misa e hincarme a rezar (to go to church and kneel to pray.)

The two or three people that were already at the bar applauded, and one whistled. She smiled and curtsied.

"Volver?" someone asked.

Just what she needed... The song took her through the process of imagining herself coming back home reluctantly, twenty years later, old and broken. Yet it ended in a note of hope:

Guardo escondida (I keep hidden)
una esperanza humilde, (a humble hope)
que es toda la fortuna (that's the whole treasure)
de mi corazón. (of my heart)

More songs were asked and given until at six the real piano player showed up and she gave away the seat, not without a pang of envy.

"You're very talented," the bartender told her when she sat at the bar.

"Thanks."

He gestured for her to approach and spoke softly in her ear, "Marry me and I'll give you a green card. You perform and I'll be your manager."

He took her by surprise. To be proposed marriage two times in a day was very bizarre. There was a lecherous shine in his eyes mixed with greed. She transformed her face into the disdainful mask she knew so well. "I already have one."

"Sure you do," the guy said, and started cleaning the bar with a cloth to look busy.

Alejandra couldn't help but see the humor of the situation. She had rejected Rob for wanting his clinic more than her, if she was honest, and here there was another guy who definitely wanted her more than his job, and she didn't accept him either. But, neither one of them loved her, they just wanted to use her.

The pianist was very good, and the singers that came later were also. She was invited to the mic by the staff and sang some tangos: *Malena, Garúa, Cambalache,* and *Naranjo en flor.*

It had been so long since she'd sung in public. She loved to perform. Time flew by and all of a sudden, Alejandra realized she was late for work. She cursed under her breath and hurried outside, calling a cab. She was going to be way late tonight, and the other transportation options were not that safe.

"Linden Boulevard Cinemas, please," she told the driver. The man looked at her in a weird way and put the car in gear.

"Late work?" he asked.

"Yeah, gotta make a living," she answered, fruitlessly trying to mimic the local accent.

When they were about two blocks from the destination, the guy parked and turned to look at her. She automatically searched for the pepper spray in her purse and unlocked the door. He showed his palms as a sign of peace. "I just wanted to let you know there's going to be a raid tonight. They are looking for illegal immigrants. We were told to stay away from the area."

"Let's get out of here before they close up," she said hurriedly.

"Where to?"

"I don't know. Back to Manhattan."

She hastily pulled her phone out and called Greg.

"You're late," were his first words.

"I know, listen..."

"If I don't see your ass coming in right this minute, don't bother to come at all. I'm sick of you playing little princess on us."

His words were harsh, but the anger in his voice was what hit her the most. It was an ultimatum. And if she accepted this treatment, she would have to accept everything else. Her jaw trembled and her eyes covered in tears. *I'm not gonna cry.* "I just wanted to let you know there will be a raid tonight. Better take the stowaways out."

"Oh, shit. I thought… Look, girl, I'm sorry… I'm just jealous, alright?"

Alejandra gathered her wits and her dignity and covered herself with it as a mantle.

"I'm terribly sorry if I lead you on. I never meant to. I'll find another job and another place to stay. I will not be bothering you anymore," she choked out and hung up.

"We're crossing the bridge now," the driver told her. "Where to?"

"Bellevue Hospital Center."

She found Rob snoring softly. It brought a small smile to her lips.

"Hey…" The noise of the chair woke him up. "What are you doing here?"

"I'll take the job if it's still available."

He took her hand and closed his eyes again. "It certainly is."

"But only the job."

"Alright." He smiled and pet her hand softly.

Chapter 11

Rob

"So, what do you think?" Rob asked eagerly when they entered his apartment. The living room was bigger than two apartments in Alejandra's building put together. She walked to the oversized windows and opened the blinds, finding a spectacular view of the Hudson River.

"Breathtaking," she answered honestly.

"I'm glad you approve." His cheeky smile made her giggle.

She looked around, unsure of what to do next. A set of leather sofas big enough to sleep on took up the main space. Over to the right, a dining table for eight people was close to a wall covered in family pictures framed in glass. On the rear wall, a tan marble breakfast bar divided the family area from the spotless, never-used-kind-of-clean kitchen. On the other side, there were several doors, all closed.

Overall, the place was comfortable but somewhat Spartan. Considering that Rob's father had talked about problems with spending, she'd expected something a lot more baroque.

"So, where is the spare bedroom?"

"There isn't one." He grinned.

She put hands on hips. "I'm not sleeping with you."

"Then the couch will have to do." He sighed loudly. "I would give you the bed, but still being broken, you know, I can't."

"Rob, I'm serious."

"Me too. There are two spare bedrooms, but they're full to the ceiling with my collectibles."

Alejandra gawked at him and walked to the first door. That one was the master bedroom. The whole room was decorated in bronze colors, a tad dark but very elegant.

When she tried to open the second door, it was blocked by a box. She pushed harder and a basketball fell on her head.

"Ouch," she complained.

"Be careful with that! It's an authentic NBA ball signed by Michael Jordan."

She gawked at him, again. "Thanks, Rob for your concern. I'm not hurt," she said.

"That ball is worth one month of your salary," he said seriously.

"This?" She took the ball to give it a closer look. "You've got to be kidding me..."

"I'm not," Rob answered. His face was neutral, but the vein of the side of his neck was ticking.

"And you have stuff in this bedroom..." Alejandra lifted one eyebrow and tilted her head.

"And the second one," he corrected.

She carefully peeked inside. It reminded her of the tango *Cambalache*. She almost expected to see a Bible slain by a saber, sitting next to a heater. The whole space was covered by all kinds of different things from different eras, mixed up in a tangle. There were old books and swords, baseball memorabilia and small furniture; closed boxes, paintings, coins and even something that looked like an Egyptian artifact.

Alejandra gaped at him, stunned.

"And the other bedroom..."

"More of the same. I'm running out of space," added Rob, evidently more relaxed.

She blinked a couple of times. "Haven't you thought about buying some shelves?"

Rob scratched the back of his neck with his healthy hand, embarrassed.

"Yeah, but, funnily enough, I only think about it when something new arrives, and by then my bank account is empty."

"Oh, dear..." Alex muttered.

* * *

Alejandra

"Are you sure about this?" Greg asked, placing the last travel bag by the door. He looked worried, in a brotherly way.

Alejandra felt her eyes filling with tears.

"Yes."

"Ok. Nice place, by the way," he added, looking at Rob, who simply nodded back.

"Yeah," she said, biting her tongue. She didn't want to mention that both spare rooms were floor to ceiling filled with expensive junk and she would have to sleep on the couch.

"Alright, I guess this is it..."

"Greg, I want to thank you for all you guys did for me, and I also want to apologize. I'm sorry if I did anything to make you think..."

He laughed with a dash of sadness. "You didn't, but a guy can only wish. God, you are a *hot, hot cupcake.*"

He widened his eyes and dangled his tongue out as if he were a dog panting.

"Stop it!" Alejandra giggled and patted his arm.

He hugged her a bit tighter and longer than proper, nodded once at Rob, who was watching the whole scene with an unreadable expression and left.

"What?" she asked Ron, after closing the door.

"That guy was with you at the club..."

"Yes. He and his girlfriend were my roommates," she answered defensively. Was he jealous?

"And?" he encouraged her.

"They had this fantasy of making a trio and waited for me for months. It never happened. When he saw us in the club, well, he didn't take it well."

She shrugged.

Rob nodded slowly. "And this is why you're here?"

Alejandra sighed and let herself fall on the sofa.

"Partly... I don't know why I'm here, but I'm willing to find out."

She gifted him with a small smile, which he answered with a full grin.

"Good enough for me. Can I have a kiss?"

"Of course not! I'm working."

"Damn!"

Alejandra looked around, hands on hips. "Where do I put my clothes? Do you have a linen closet around here?"

"Everything's full," he answered sheepishly.

"Alright, I think I'll call Greg then. Evidently, there is no room here for me..."

"Wait! There's plenty of space in my bedroom closet. I don't keep clothes for long."

Alejandra opened his wall to wall closet to find it half empty. Everything was pristine and organized. Five work jackets, five pants and five shirts covered his workdays, and there were also half a dozen other variants for special occasions.

"This is very bizarre..." Alejandra commented.

"I'm an orderly guy in everything but my collection."

"Have you ever visited a psychologist about it?"

"No need... I know exactly where my craziness comes from. My father traveled for months at a time when I was a child. He used to bring me presents from every trip, but he didn't let me play with them. They were precious and needed to be *collected*. I guess every time I buy something new, I try to replay those feelings of being briefly loved. Unfortunately, I also get the turbulent emotions that come afterwards. To make things even more interesting, for the last fifteen years more or less, my mother has become a nomad. Now she is the one bringing me pieces from abroad."

"Oh…"

"So… you can move all my stuff to this half and keep the other half to yourself. They're separate. That way I don't freak out if you are messy."

"Freak out?"

"Yeah… I've lived alone for the past twenty years, sweetheart. This might be challenging for me."

Alejandra skimmed the place, thoughtfully. "Twenty years, that's a lot…how old are you?"

"Thirty-eight. And you? Can you tell?"

Alejandra chuckled. "I'm twenty-seven and I've never lived alone."

Rob's brows sled upwards. "Always lived with roommates after leaving home? Or partners?"

She shook her head.

"I was at my parents' home right until I moved here. And then it was Greg and Sam."

Rob's forehead ridged, but he didn't say anything.

"It's quite normal in my country, alright? Why spend money on a rental when you can save it and later on buy a place of your own?" She quipped defensively.

"So everyone is a homeowner?" Rob sat on the bed.

"Not everyone, but that's the culturally accepted thing to do." Alejandra folded her arms.

"Interesting, and different. So… about that kiss?" He said palming the bed next to him.

"Not gonna happen."

"Damn…"

Chapter 12

Rob

When Rob saw Alejandra's toothbrush in his bathroom, something clicked in his mind. There was a woman in his house. There was a woman in his life. He hadn't noticed how empty his life had been until now. He'd thought it would be difficult, and he knew it might be at some point, but so far it was pure joy.

The mirror showed his mother's reflection by the door. She was smiling.

"Let's get you dressed. Hack and Janice are already here."

He maneuvered the electric wheelchair out of the bathroom and into his bedroom.

"Thanks, but I can manage."

"I'm glad. Let me see."

"Mom...I'm not a child anymore," he whined.

"Good. About time," his mother said, a hint of a smirk lifting the corner of her mouth.

Rob chuckled. He was an oversized little kid in his parent's eyes, wasn't he? *Well, no way to argue with the truth...* He tried to maneuver his polo shirt around the arm cast and his head with no avail.

"I guess you have a solution." He gazed at her with one eye, from the buttoned opening of the shirt in which his head was completely tangled.

His mother giggled, coming to the rescue. "I do," she said, helping him take the shirt off again and handing him a neatly folded pair of basketball shorts and its accompanying shirt. "Not too elegant, but it will do."

Rob put on the shirt with ease and looked at the shorts.

"I'm going to need a rail installed," he murmured.

"Yes. Now let me help you."

"No, Mom. I'm too heavy for you. Please call Hack."

"Good idea," his mother acknowledged and left the room.

"Hey, man. Need a lil help?" Hack asked, closing the door behind him.

"Yeah, can you lift me up? I'm like a turtle upside down."

"You need a rail installed."

"I know. I'll call my father later. Won't need to change till tomorrow, so no problem."

Changing was fast and easy with an extra pair of hands.

"Thanks, man," Rob said.

"Any time, bro," Hack answered, sitting on the bed. "About the girl. Are you fucking her? She's not acting like a maid."

"Alejandra? I wish… She's from Buenos Aires."

"Oh." Hack nodded slowly a couple of times, taking in the information. "I get it now. It's the only country I've visited where the hotel staff looks you straight in the eye. Remember the time we spent there?"

"How can I forget? She's a tango dancer. My father will give me the clinic if I can convince her to marry me."

"Wow. And you want to?"

"It's a whopping improvement from Millicent."

"Anyone is better than Millicent."

"You're right about that."

Rob maneuvered the wheelchair toward the living room, just stopping to open the door.

Outside, he found Janice, Alex and his mother comfortably chatting like old friends. Janice was a beautiful, tiny thing, all delicacy and class. Alejandra was a jaw-dropping, eye-popping Valkyrie. *Kill me any time.*

Hack was right. She couldn't play a maid role even if she tried. She was a great host though. *Perfect.*

Chapter 13

Alex

Alex prepared breakfast with her neck killing her, again. She'd never considered beating eggs a challenging task, but it was right now. Sleeping on the sofa for a month was definitely not healthy. Something had to change. Fast.

"Rob," she called.

"Yes?" he said, without lifting his eyes from the iPad.

"I'm going to the mall today."

"No need to go. Give me my debit card back and we'll buy online. I've just found the most exquisite baroque jewelry box on eBay. I'm quite sure there's history behind it."

She lifted her chin.

"I'm not giving your card back, and I'm going."

"Why?" Now his eyes were on her, making her uncomfortable.

Since when was he possessive? Did he think she wanted to steal from him? Was his buying addiction kicking in? She needed some fresh air, or she would go mad.

"I haven't taken a day off in a month. I need to see people, and I want to buy an air bed. I can't take it anymore. My back is killing me."

Rob blew air through his lips, took a pen with his healthy hand and stuck it under the cast to scratch his broken arm. "You can't transform the living room into a campsite. I receive visitors here."

"Well, I can't sleep on the sofa either."

"Then come to bed. All your clothes are already in my bedroom."

"No!" Alex walked over to him and smacked his healthy arm in its scratching adventure. "Stop doing that, you're going to hurt yourself," she admonished.

Rob took the opportunity and grabbed her hand into his, catching her by surprise.

"Baby, it's time," he said, looking deep into her eyes.

Alejandra panicked—she knew she was defenseless against those eyes.

"Let go," she said.

"This is gonna hurt," he muttered and pulled hard, making her lose balance and fall on his lap. She screeched and he flinched.

Alejandra tried to get up, but he put his hand on the back of her neck and brought her to him, kissing her lips.

She pushed his chest, but he persevered until she stopped fighting and kissed him back. Alex found herself sliding into *the zone*, that place where everything was right with the world.

She was brought back to reality by a swat on her butt, a hard one.

"Ouch!" she screamed jumping away from him and smacking his healthy arm again. "What the hell was that for?"

He extended his hand.

"Do not touch me," she warned, spitting fire through her eyes. "I'm going to say this once and only once: No man has ever hit me, and if you dare to do that again, you will not have another chance. I will make sure of that." She stared at him with that look she reserved to scare men away, the one that promised sensible body parts cut off with rusty scissors.

"Sorry, but I needed to know." There was something primal and raw in his eyes, which Alex couldn't put a name on. She was not willing to find out at this time either. She was furious.

"To know what?" she asked, fists on hips.

"That you're not a masochist."

What?

"Of course I'm not a masochist!"

"Good," he said grinning. "Then you can come to bed."

She gawked, opened and closed her mouth a couple of times, and stormed out the kitchen.

* * *

Alex

Alex had been out almost all day and Rob was worried. Mr. Wilson, Hack's chief of security, was following her around, but Rob was unsettled if he didn't see her. He was sure the raid hadn't been done by chance and suspected Millicent had something to do with it. Funny enough, the raid had pushed Alex into his arms; well, not yet, but soon. *Life has an interesting sense of humor sometimes.*

He'd been waiting for this day the whole month. The day she couldn't sleep on the sofa anymore. She'd lasted longer than he'd predicted. *Stubborn and hot. Perfect.* Today had been the last test too. He needed to know she didn't enjoy pain before letting his heart run loose. Not all, but many women into pain created very destructive relationships. He suspected Millicent would enjoy a good whipping; he was not going to be the one giving it though.

A key turned in the lock, and there she was. Alex was carrying a long box that seemed heavy. Behind her, Wilson had another one.

"Over here," she pointed at the wall. "Thanks so much, Mr. Wilson. I don't know what I would've done without you."

"Not a problem, sweetheart. Not at all."

"Hubert?" Rob asked bewildered.

"Hey, Doc. You have a very clever lady here. She realized she was being followed and almost pepper-sprayed me."

Rob crackled.

"Yeah, very funny…" He looked at Alex. "I'll come tomorrow to help you put these together, alright?"

"That would be wonderful," she said and gifted the old man with a luminescent smile.

"I better get going. Have a great evening you two."

Once the door closed, Rob pointed at the boxes. "What's that?"

"Shelves," she answered flatly. "I need to change."

Alex disappeared into the bedroom and opened the door ten minutes later with a tank top, spandex pants, and a bandana covering her hair.

"What are you doing," Rob asked panicked when he saw her opening one of the spare bedrooms' doors.

"I'm going to organize your *collectibles*, so I can take one room."

"You can't mess with my stuff like this!" his voice rose into an annoying, high-pitched tone.

"Watch me," she answered, putting fists on hips.

* * *

Rob

She'd said *Watch me*, and that's what Rob did. The first hour, with his teeth clenched and the nerves on edge, waiting for the moment she broke something to fire her and kick her presumptuous ass out of his life. But she didn't. She touched everything with major care and organized the pieces neatly, cleaning them with a dry cloth in the process.

The second hour he relaxed enough to enjoy the view and analyze his own feelings. He wanted this woman so much it hurt. He needed her to have his clinic, yet he'd been a split second from grabbing her by the arm and taking her out. Were his possessions so important? Possessions he never gave a second look at?

The more he saw her muscles flexing under the spandex the more he forgot how much he cared for his stuff. He hadn't noticed before how muscular she was. Not in a bodybuilder way, but in a ballerina way. She was a hot looking woman, and she was his for the taking. If only she could want all of him and not just the Dom. He sighed. *That's too much to ask.*

By three am, she hadn't taken out more than half of the stuff from the first bedroom, and she was starting to look dazed.

"Alright," he said coming closer with the wheelchair. "Let's go now."

"Where?" she asked, trying to fight, but she had no strength left.

"Bed."

"But…"

"I can't do much until they take the casts out." He signaled the plastic pieces that immobilized his leg and arm.

"Just sleep?"

He smiled.

Chapter 14

Alex

Alejandra took a shower and almost crawled to the bed, that's how tired she was. Rob was propped on the pillows looking at her with devilish eyes.

"C'mere," he said, and she reluctantly obeyed, putting her head on his shoulder. He massaged her back and she relaxed in his embrace.

"Rob?"

"Yes, sweetheart."

"I can't take a salary anymore if I'm going to sleep with you."

He kissed the top of her head. "Alright, let's call it backup savings, in case I go crazy and spend everything in my account. Does it work?"

"Yes, it works." She smiled into his chest.

"How are we doing, by the way? Did we manage to save anything? I can't believe I let you confiscate my cards."

She giggled. "Almost everything actually. Your dad pays all the expenses, and Janice has been sending us the food."

"Mmm," he said, making figure-eights with his fingers on her back. "You're a miracle worker."

His hand trailed lower along her spine.

"You promised, just sleep…" she complained but curved her back.

"That was before you accepted sleeping with me long term," his index finger fondled her tail bone, making the small hairs of her back to bristle.

"I didn't." Her head bounced up and her eyes looked directly into his.

He brought his healthy hand from its expedition and led her face back into his chest.

"Yes, when you told me you couldn't receive a salary anymore now that you were sleeping with me."

His fingers feathered along her arm.

"Mmm..." It felt so good to be in his arms. It felt more than good; it felt right. Alex realized it was time. She let out a deep sigh where she surrendered the last shreds of her resistance and nuzzled his nipple.

Rob gave a shaky sigh himself.

Alejandra looked into his eyes, and he smiled.

His hand went to her nape, "Kiss me," he murmured.

She knew what was coming.

"Are you sure? You are hurt."

He pressed the nape of her neck and her lips touched his. He kissed her slowly, savoring the moment.

"I can't do much, but you can," he said between kisses. "God, you are so beautiful, let me see all of you."

She pulled back and rose to her knees, taking her oversized t-shirt off. Now she was down to her panties.

"All of it," he said, and she obeyed, taking her panties off.

He looked at her admiringly and his hand went to her right breast. "So pink. C'mere, let me taste."

Alejandra grabbed the headboard for support and lowered her chest close to his face. His hand went to one of her peaks and she felt his mouth closing around her nipple. He feasted on her and she slowly slid into the zone. His touch had instructions that she followed, a small pressure to the side made her move and offer her other breast to his mouth, a squeeze of her buttocks made her press forward.

He played with her like this for a long time, learning her body and letting her learn his. She fell deeper and deeper into a trance, and her pussy started to pulse from time to time.

He nuzzled the skin between her breasts. "It's time. Second drawer, on the left."

Alex licked his neck and moved out of the bed. She went to the second drawer and there it was, a package of condoms.

She looked at herself in the mirror above the dresser.

Did she really want this? *Yes.*

Her hands ripped the packet open and she put the condom in her mouth, with the little bubble to the inside.

When she turned, Rob lifted one eyebrow. It probably looked as if she had a pacifier in her mouth. She smiled a naughty smile, climbed onto the bed and moved the sheet away. He was naked and fully erect.

Her hands caressed the base of his shaft while her mouth went to the tip. She placed the condom and rolled it down with her lips and tongue. Rob pushed his hips upwards due to the stimulation, and a shadow of pain crossed his face.

She straddled him and moved forward for a kiss. "Now it's your time to stay still," she murmured in his ear. He fisted her hair and kissed her passionately, plunging his tongue inside her until she lost all cockiness and became putty again. Only then did he let her go.

"Ride me," he breathed.

She took a second to collect her emotions and feel him. Positioning his shaft at her entrance, she sat on him. She felt full and expanded.

He sighed.

"Look at me," he commanded, and his hand went to her hip.

She did, and his eyes were deep and hypnotic again. His hand squeezed one time and she started moving in a long circular motion. She could feel the base of his shaft pressing on the lips of her pussy and her clit. He squeezed again and she gained speed, getting lost in the feelings, in the ride.

"C'mere."

Without disengaging she approached him and kissed him. He fisted her hair again and kissed her hard, desperately. She responded to his needs, her needs. Her nub was being stimulated more fully now.

"Faster," he commanded.

She did and found the spot of maximum stimulation.

"You've got it, sweets. Go for it."

His hand went to her breast and squeezed, while she was lost in the sensations.

"Come for me," he rumbled.

Her body went crazy with need and she let it loose. She gyrated, and pushed, and squeezed until she emitted a long loud moan and her body convulsed.

"Stay," he commanded through gritted teeth.

He was very close. Alejandra sat back and clenched the muscles of her passage, stimulating him. She could do it at will. He opened his eyes, surprised, and grunted, releasing his seed.

Chapter 15

Alex

The tune sounded familiar and eased into a dream where Alex was walking naked over the wires of San Francisco's bridge. In the dream, the music gave her wings and she danced and flew over the treacherous border with abandon. She felt free. As the tune advanced, she stirred and finally woke up in Rob's bed.

He wasn't by her side and the melody came from the living room. The piece being played was *El Choclo*, the first tango they danced together. It wasn't a recording.

Still naked under her nightdress, Alex walked toward the music. There it was Rob, actually playing the harmonica.

"It's good to have my hand again," he wiggled his fingers at her and grinned. They had taken off the cast the day before and he'd been exulting the rest of the day, squeezing her butt at every turn, mischief never leaving his eyes. Alejandra had realized at that point she was going to see a lot more of the real Rob now.

She sat on the sofa. "I was wondering... where did you learn to dance the tango?"

He smiled. "I took ballroom dancing classes. It included tango. And then Hack and I went to Argentina on a field trip. Hack took polo lessons, and I chose tango."

"A field trip? Wow. What kind of school gives international field trips?"

"We were home-schooled. My mother loves to travel, so she managed to do everything at the same time."

"She is a clever lady," Alejandra mused.

"That she is." Old memories seemed to surface drawing a tender smile on his face.

"Tell me about Hack. You seem very close."

"His house was right by ours. I never really asked what happened, but my mother took him in almost at the same time his mother left. I was about three and he was five. His father traveled a lot, so he pretty much lived with us. He's more of a brother to me than my own."

"I love my brothers. They're the best."

Silence extended between them.

"C'mere…"

"What?" She arched one eyebrow.

"Oh, is that how it is? I was going to play a tune for you, but that sass deserves something different."

"Like what?" She asked with a twinkle in her eyes.

"Sit on my face?" He doubled down.

"You are so…" she growled, taking one of the pillows and throwing it at him.

He caught it with his good arm, laughing. His not so good arm extended toward her.

Alejandra sighed and snuggled by his side. He helped her slide down until her head was on his lap and her body lay on the couch.

"Want me to play a tune?"

"Yes, please."

He combed his fingers through her hair once and breathed in her scent. "I love your perfume."

"It's jasmine."

"Lovely."

The tune started and she was transported back home to one of the lazy evenings at the beach. Her parents had a small vacation house in

Mar de las Pampas where she spent most of her summer holidays as a child. There was always someone with a guitar, and this song was one of the favorites. *La Llave* (The key) was the name, and it was a pledge from a lonely guy missing his lady, dreaming of the time when she would enter his home without asking for the key.

Alex knew the song by heart, and singing was just natural.

Rob seemed confused for a second, but he caught on quickly, playing the tune with even more heart than before.

When he finished, Alejandra took the harmonica away from his mouth and planted a kiss there instead.

"Woman, you sing."

"I know," she answered only to kiss him again.

He encased her face with both hands and rained kisses on her cheeks and forehead before going back to her mouth.

"I mean... you can really sing."

Alejandra found it amusing, in a hot way. "Yes, Rob, I sing. I took acting classes and I play the piano too. Are you going to kiss me or what?"

He grinned.

"What," he said, wiggling his eyebrows.

"Oh..." Stretching like a cat, she lifted herself and sat on her heels over the sofa.

"Bring the mirror from the entrance and place it on the couch looking at us."

"What?"

"C'mon. It's going to be fun."

Alejandra followed his directions. "You have a voyeur streak?"

"I'm an eternal explorer of pleasure... and the night at the club, I would've given anything to see your beautiful face spiraling into bliss. I want to fulfill that dream now."

"Oh..." Alejandra felt a tug in her chest that was hard to describe without using the big L-word.

"Sit on my lap, facing out."

She straddled him, eager to please.

"Mmm you smell so good..." he inhaled deeply into her neck, giving her goosebumps.

Her body squirmed, and she looked into the mirror. There she could see those eyes, the ones that knew all the secrets of the universe, assessing her reactions. She felt studied, but lovingly so, and cherished like never before.

His hands went to her breasts and massaged them over the satin of her nightdress. Alejandra closed her eyes, relaxed her body and put her head on his shoulder.

"Oh, yes, so pretty."

His left thumb trailed slowly down, while the back of the fingers on his right hand moved deliberately to the outer side of her breast.

"Tell me, are you ticklish?"

"Mmm?"

"Lift your arms..."

His fingertips crawled excruciatingly gently toward her armpit. Alejandra held it until she couldn't anymore and put her arm down, enclosing his hand. Her whole body trembled. "Stop."

"So sensitive... one day I'm going to tie you up and make you come just with a feather."

"I don't think I'd like that."

His hand was back on her breast, massaging tenderly.

"To be tied up or the feather?"

"Neither, I like my freedom, and I love your hands."

"Thanks for letting me know. Now, what do we have here?"

His other hand was already all the way between her legs and closed around her vulva.

Alejandra's hips buckled. "Oh..."

The spaghetti straps slid down her shoulders and her breasts came into view, then it was the time for the hem of her dress to drift upwards leaving her completely exposed. She looked into the mirror and their image.

"See how beautiful you are?"

She smiled and let her head fall on his shoulder again.

"Rob?"

"Yes, sweetheart?"

His fingertips were drawing lazy arabesques on her skin, seeking the path of sensory stimulation. His eyes never leaving her.

"I want you inside…"

"You want me to lose control?"

"Yes…" she acknowledged, her colors rising.

He nodded once, smiled secretively, and nuzzled her neck.

"Your wish is my command."

His hands left her body, leaving a ghostly ache behind, and she saw in their reflection how he retrieved a condom.

"May I?" she asked.

"Of course…"

Alejandra moved away, avoiding his still-injured leg, and unwrapped the rubbery material. She fell onto her knees and licked his already freed rod thoroughly, before placing the condom on the head and rolling it down slowly.

"Oh, gorgeous…"

With the ease of a cat, she straddled him again as before and sank her sleek passage around his manhood. A mischievous smile crossed her face before she started clenching her inner muscles.

"Is that so?" he said, shivering.

One of his hands went right to her clit, all finesse forgotten. The other one pulled at her nipple and his mouth sucked in her neck.

She convulsed under the sudden stimulation.

The image reflected by the mirror was pure, unadulterated sin.

"Move, sweets. See if you can make me come before you do," he challenged.

Alex took the bait and rode him with abandon. The harder she tried, the more she was sucked into the zone, and she didn't even notice when she lost all control.

His fingers played piano with her clit and pressure in her underbelly built up to tidal wave proportions. His eyes never left her, his hands never left her, and she felt compelled to go further, to feel further, to share further.

Until the wave smashed on the shore, leaving her in an altered state of bliss, electrified and sedated at the same time.

A triumphant grin spread across Rob's face and he finally let go, falling back onto the sofa.

Chapter 16

Rob looked at his leg and smirked. "Well, hello there," he greeted the pale skin and bony calf. He couldn't complain though. It had healed in record time and the cast had just been removed, eight weeks after the accident. His arm, with an even faster recovery, was looking almost normal.

The body's inner wisdom was really astonishing. He knew that bones didn't exactly heal, they regenerated—our own version of the salamanders growing a new leg. And for that, they needed the proper building materials. There had been a squabble in the hospital when he declined the metal screws and asked the bones to just be repositioned. They only capitulated when he threatened to sue them for malpractice citing papers assessing the long-term effects of both procedures. Or maybe it had been Hack and Renton's threatening stance. He didn't know, but he was thankful.

After trying Janice's food and seeing the results, he started to understand firsthand how things really worked. He'd never learned in medical school how to support bone re-growth. Only found out about it after taking functional medicine courses. Janice had been kind enough to tweak her recipes to oblige his needs. Amazing what bone broth could do.

Alex came from the kitchen biting a pen. "What?" she asked when she realized he was watching her.

"I'm just wondering how the hell I got so lucky."

Beaming, she came to him. He sat her on his lap and went for a kiss.

"What are you doing?" he inquired.

"I'm looking into the list of materials for the clinic, trying to estimate the total costs."

"And?"

"Mmm…"

"Bad?"

"About a hundred thousand…"

"And we have?"

"Twenty thousand."

"There's no way, then. My father did it again, didn't he? Set me up for failure…" Rob felt angry and deceived.

"Mmm…"

Alex's smiling, what are the odds? "Mmm, what?"

"There is a way, I think."

"Really? How?"

"Have you ever made an inventory of your collection?"

There we go again…

"No way in hell I give up my collection!" He pouted, literally.

Alex rolled her eyes.

"You didn't answer my question. Do you have an inventory?" she asked nonchalantly.

"No," he answered grumpily and centered his attention in a tiny stain on the wood floors.

"Well, I finished organizing the stuff on shelves, and there are lots of things there. It could probably buy you a clinic of your own."

"I'm not giving up my collection, period," he repeated, stubbornly.

Alex sighed. "Ok, you'll have to start smaller then and grow the materials as people come in. Not a big deal. Most of the expensive stuff is not exactly necessary; you can send the patients elsewhere to do it."

"How do you know all this?" After the emotional roller-coaster, Rob realized she had done a heck of a job.

"I never told you? My second brother is a dentist. I helped him sometimes at the office."

"Let me get this straight. You're a ballet dancer and a tango dancer. You're a pretty good singer and pianist. You've got experience as a secretary. Why on earth were you cleaning movie theaters when we first met?"

"Cleaning, construction, farming, landscaping, elder care, babysitting… and porn…" She made a face, "are the only jobs you can get without a work permit. All the other doors are locked."

"There must be so much wasted talent…"

"There is."

"That's a shame."

"Yes, and no. I don't think it's bad to protect your own people. It's easy to jump in a boat that's already floating, not so much to push it into the water."

"Well, but those of us enjoying the nice floating boat are not the ones who pushed it in, to begin with."

"True. Yet I'm quite sure they made the sacrifice thinking of their own grandchildren."

He sighed. "So, you're saying that if we keep saving, we can open the clinic with only what my father is giving us?"

"Pretty much, yes. I still think you need to catalog and create an inventory of your junk. That way, if there is something important you need to buy fast, you know what pieces to sell."

"It's not junk, and I'm not selling it. Period."

She rolled her eyes again. "Alrighty then."

* * *

Alex

Alex couldn't believe her eyes. She was on the rooftop of Hack's building, walking in a small fruit forest; petite trees and bushes creating an enchanting landscape.

"Janice, this is beautiful," she told Hack's fiancé and creator of the garden. They were invited for dinner to celebrate that Rob's casts were off.

"Thanks," Janice answered. "There's a pond over there, and we can sit."

Alex agreed with a bright smile.

"Fish too? I can't believe what you've done here."

"Hack knows I love edible landscaping, so he facilitated this. It keeps me happy and busy."

"What do you mean by edible landscaping? Everything here can be eaten?"

Alex looked around, her mouth drawing a perfect O, and her eyes huge.

"Not all, but most, yes." Janice also looked at her small piece of paradise with a secretive smile.

"The food you sent us..."

"Yes, all from here."

"Thanks so much. It was delicious. Rob is sure it sped up his recovery."

"Really? Wow." Janice's proud grin spread across her face. She was truly happy. "Do you cook?"

"I'm a very bad cook. Steak, fries and salad are all I can do." Alex chuckled.

Janice smiled, playing with her engagement ring.

"So, engaged, hum?" Alex asked, looking at the diamond.

"Well..." Janice pursed her lips and twisted them to one side. "It has a GPS in it so Hack can locate me at all times. It's better than being microchipped."

Alejandra laughed. "He wouldn't dare..."

"Oh yeah, he would. He actually mentioned it." Janice chuckled.

"And how does it make you feel?" Confusion clouded Alex's face for a second.

"It's unacceptable, but what can I do? I can't be mad at Hack for long. It's just his way to show how much he cares. Marcos is still out there. I think the only reason he didn't attack again is because my caveman belongs to a meaner cartel." She rolled her eyes and giggled.

"Cartel? Which cartel?"

"Military-industrial complex. His family is deep into that funky stuff. So, how are you doing with Rob?" Janice hastily changed the subject.

"Oh… Rob wants to get married. It's one of the conditions his father is forcing on him." Alejandra sighed.

"And you want to marry him?"

"Crazy as it sounds, I think I do."

"Then? Are you playing hard to get?"

"It is not that I want to give him a hard time. It's just that it's too soon and I don't know what he really feels about me. I don't think something as sacred as marriage should be a means to an end, part of a business."

"He does love you, you know? Even though he is too scared to acknowledge it."

"You think?" Alejandra sighed. "I need him to say it and mean it. So far, he has talked about the clinic and about giving me a green card. I can't make a lifelong commitment for any of those reasons."

"Well, I hope you work it out. You're made for each other."

Alejandra smiled, her eyes misty. "How about you? Why are you giving Hack a hard time?"

Janice shook her head. "My mother came to visit two months ago and asked me the same question… I just don't want to go through the ceremony."

"Why?"

"I don't know all the reasons. I'm kind of avoiding that particular conversation with myself. I do know that the idea of my father and

Hack's father sitting at the same table gives me goosebumps, and not in a good way."

"Then skip the party or seat them at separate tables. You don't want them to meet at all?"

Janice sighed. "Think about it. Think what Hack's family's money could do for my father's career. He could be the next president of Colombia."

"Hmmm. And that's bad because…?"

"Because my father is not a nice person, Alejandra, and Hack's father is not a nice person either. And these guys never give money away. They invest and expect high returns, and their business always implies people dying."

"I see your point…" whispered Alejandra, thoughtfully.

"There is something else…" Janice said, fidgeting with the hem of her shirt.

Alejandra watched her intently.

"Due to all this mess, I left the decision to fate. If I get pregnant, we get married, and if I don't, well, we don't."

"And?"

"It's eight months we are together, we are not taking any precautions and I'm not conceiving."

"Oh."

"Yeah, oh and a half. I went to see Hack's doctor. He ran some tests and said there was nothing physical involved. He hinted it was because I didn't feel safe, so my body was playing tricks."

"Is it possible?"

"In my case, yes. Every time I didn't want to go to school as a child, I would get an asthma attack."

"Oh, wow. Those are scary."

"They are."

"And that's the reason behind the ring?"

"Yes, Hack tries to solve my psychological problems with money and technology. Therefore the forest on the top of the roof to relax me and keep me busy, and the ring so I feel safe."

"Is it working?"

Janice bit her lip and shook her head. The young woman took a deep breath, hit her knees with her palms and stood up. "How about picking up some yellow tomatoes for the salad?"

"You have them here too?" Alejandra grinned, but her eyes were still foggy.

Janice nodded, forcing herself to smile.

* * *

Rob

"Any news?" Rob asked Hack when the women were upstairs.

"Yeah..." Hack put on a sour face.

"That bad?"

"I still don't know, but I don't like the way it looks."

"Do tell."

Hack opened a hidden door in the side of his breakfast bar and retrieved two whiskey glasses and a bottle. He placed the glasses on the living room table and poured a generous amount of the amber liquid in each of them.

"I've been following both Millicent and Roger."

"And?" Rob pushed his lips together into a thin line. *I'm not gonna like this.*

"They're lovers. Well, they fuck. She's very upset at him for something he did, though, and put him in the freezer. She said that, quote, *his irrational jealousy almost ruined everything and that she would not take it,* end quote. That's as far as they got on the phone."

"Are you thinking what I'm thinking?"

"That the sleazy scumbag tried to kill you? Yeah. I'm digging deeper under that assumption."

Rob whistled. "Anything else?"

"Yes. She's the local CEO of Bymex LLC now, the pharmaceutical company we've been talking about."

"Oh shit..."

"And there's more."

Rob sighed. "More?"

"Your father is on the board of directors."

Oh...

"Since when?"

"Six months ago. He bought enough shares to get a seat."

"That's probably the price he paid to have the bitch agree to marry me. He said it hadn't been cheap."

"Pretty fucked up. I worry about your lady with all these sharks around."

"Me too," Rob agreed.

"I have something for you."

Hack took a jewelry box from a drawer and slid it to Rob.

"I'm not marrying you," Rob said, smirking.

"Not funny." Hack laughed. "It has a GPS in it. Make Alex wear it at all times."

"Perfect. Now I only need her to say *yes*."

"What are the odds? I'm making progress with Janice. I think that if we just fly to Vegas, she'll go for it."

"I don't know. It seems like Alex wants to, but she's waiting for something. I'm running out of ideas."

"Being a sub, she should be all starry-eyed. Is she not?"

"A sub? With her hot temper and quirkiness? Not in a million years. She just slides in the zone easily because of her tango training, but it only happens when *dancing*."

"Oh..." said Hack, and both men nodded in tandem.

"Do you know the last crazy thing that woman came up with?"

Hack lifted his eyebrows, waiting for his friend to go on.

"She wants me to catalog my collection in case I need to sell something, and she called it *junk*." Rob let his indignation show.

Hack snorted.

"Not funny, man." Rob chuckled, "Well, it is. Just a little."

"I think it's a great idea," Hack said.

"What? What side are you on?"

"It's not about sides. It's about knowing what you have. Right now, anyone can steal from you and you won't even notice."

"You have a point there. How do you catalog a collection?"

"There's an appraiser who takes care of acquisitions for me. I can send him over."

"How much does the guy charge? We're saving like squirrels in the fall."

Hack smiled. "Don't worry about it. My treat."

Chapter 17

Alex

"I have something for you," Rob said when they were getting ready for bed, showing Alex the jewelry box in his hand.

"Does it have a GPS?" Alex's pretty mouth drew into a lopsided grin, which was almost a smirk.

"Hmmm yeah…" Rob pulled his lower lip upwards, his personal way to pout.

"Let me see," she encouraged.

He opened the box and there it was: a gorgeous engagement ring with a multifaceted diamond.

"It's beautiful. Hack has great taste."

Rob's eyes were fixed on the sheets of the bed, avoiding hers.

"I'll use it, so you know where I am. I'm still not marrying you."

"Why the hell not?" Now he was staring at her, a hurt shadow in his eyes.

"Because you never said you loved me…"

"I…"

"Don't. It's too late to say it now that I told you. I could never believe you."

Rob sighed. "Woman, what do you want from me?"

"I just want you to love me…"

"Don't you think it is a bit early to talk about love?"

"Yes, but not as early as to talk about marriage."

He huffed. "Every single second that you're here without a green card, you're in danger of being deported... Look, I just don't want to lose you, ok? I...just marry me. We'll figure out the rest later."

"It doesn't work that way, you know. If we get married and I'm already illegal, I'll be permanently banned."

"I don't understand. How is Hack going to do it?"

"Janice came walking. He can fly her out of the country and marry in Mexico, for example. Then bring her in legally. Besides, she is the daughter of a senator. Politicians are the new royalty. They are above the law."

"All doesn't matter. Hack will find a way for us as well. Please?"

She shook her head and took a deep breath.

"Maybe I can't say I love you yet, but I do like you a lot," he pressed.

"I know you like me a lot. I know you wouldn't consider it too much of a hassle to spend some years, maybe the rest of your life with me."

He smiled and opened his hands, palms up, encouraging her to keep going.

"But..."

"There we go..." he muttered.

"You don't love me more than your clinic. You don't love me more than your junk. If you ever had to choose, I would be last."

"What do you want from me? You want me to let go of my life? And be, what? Your lapdog?"

"Of course not!"

"Then?"

"You know what? Never mind... you wouldn't understand."

Alejandra passed her necklace chain through the ring with shaky hands and clicked the chain again. The necklace already had a pendant of the child Virgin Mary. Now the ring was right beside it.

"There. Happy? Now you know where I am all the times."

She got up and went to the bathroom, turning the shower on. It had been her private space since she came to live with Rob, the place where he couldn't follow because of the casts. When she was under the water, Rob came into the bathroom.

"What?" she spat.

"This," he answered, entering the shower.

She looked at him, standing on his two legs now, and sighed.

"You are not going to leave me alone, are you?"

"Do you really want me to?" His eyes were deep, wise, as if he knew all the secrets of the universe. How could he be a spoiled, self-centered ass one second and this the next? She closed her eyes and pressed her back to the wall of the shower, defeated.

Alejandra felt his fingers trailing her waist while his lips pressed softly over hers.

"I spoke with my father today," he murmured while raining kisses on her neck.

"When?" she asked, whimpering a little.

"Before going to Hack's." He pulled her earlobe into his mouth.

"And?" She moaned.

"He'll help with the clinic with what we have now. No need to get married."

Alejandra opened her eyes, sobering. "And you still gave me the ring?"

He put both hands on the sides of her head and gave her a small peck on the lips. "Yes."

He touched her forehead with his. "It's too early to talk about love, but I feel we have something very special going on. I know I'm complicated and somewhat risky, but you bring out the best in me and keep the bad parts in check. I know I can be good for you too. We're great together; don't you see it? Please give me a chance."

Happy tears streamed down her face. "Let's do this. If, after the clinic is up and running, we still feel like this, then we get married. Ok?"

"Thanks, baby…"

He pressed his lips to hers again, firmly this time, and she melted in his embrace.

"You know? There is something I wanted to do since the first time we danced," he breathed in her ear while his thumb caressed her sensitive peak and his other hand squeezed her behind.

"Mmm, what?"

"Put your foot on my shoulder…"

"Oh." She lifted her knee to the side and only then straightened the leg, making an almost perfect one-eighty.

He looked down at her completely exposed core.

"Oh gorgeous, this is so hot!"

Chapter 18

Rob

Rob assessed every detail in the place one more time and sighed. It was not what he'd envisioned when imagining his new clinic, but it would have to do for now. It was a small place, with two rooms plus bathroom and kitchen. The front room was the reception slash waiting room, and the second one was the office. To make things even worse, it was located all the way at the back of the nine-story clinic his father had built for his former employers, right by the dumpsters and employee parking lot. He would have to add a map and detailed instructions to any flyer, and the most likely outcome was to send business to the competition.

Alejandra had been happy with it. She'd said: "A caballo regalado no se le miran los dientes," which Rob hadn't understood. It was "horse something, something teeth." No way to make any sense of it.

His father had bent his requirements and gave him space, even though he was not married. Rob was not sure whether to be happy or worried about this sudden change. The old man had always been extremely inflexible in his conditions.

But, all in all, they had made it. Today was the big day. Sparkling wine was flowing among the invitees, and everyone was having a good time. Alejandra and Janice were buzzing in a corner, with Hack keeping an eye on them. A good friend, who was an aspiring painter, had brought some of his artwork and a Hungarian girl, who was friends with Alex from her former work at the cinema, was playing the space drums. Rob had never heard them before; the sound was otherworldly.

He felt a cold breath on the nape of his neck and looked out the entrance. Millicent had just arrived. She stayed by the door as if expecting life to stop and everyone to watch her. There was a flash from a photographer, and some people went to greet her.

Rob purposely ignored her. Walking toward Alex, he hugged her from behind and nuzzled her neck. The time secluded in his apartment had been a good parenthesis from the nasty business between them and the clinic, but apparently, life was about to push forward in all its awkwardness.

What was Millicent doing here? He hadn't invited her, nor had answered her messages. Didn't this woman have any dignity? Or was it all just business?

"I see playing with ditch diggers has clouded your sense of decorum. I'm your fiancé. You're supposed to come to me in public, not hug your little whore."

Rob's veins went thick, and his hands closed into fists. His head turned toward her face, without releasing Alex, who was frozen in place.

"Get out before I call the police. You're not invited, nor are you welcome. Out. Now."

"Or what? Oh yes… you're going to call the police. Please do. I would like to see you explain why you're hiding illegal immigrants and exploiting them."

Rob gawked.

"Why don't you go around the building, and up to the seventh floor? There, you'll find Roger, your little boy toy," Hack interceded, smirking.

"I have no idea what you're talking about," Millicent said, losing her aplomb.

"You know there are no secrets I can't unravel," Hack pressed.

Her nostrils flared. She broke eye contact with Hack and looked at Rob again. "You will marry me because it's been arranged between the families, and there's no going back. You'll forget this stupid game of playing modern medicine-man and do the right thing. You'll see…"

She looked at Alejandra. "And you, you little rat… You're short, ugly, stupid and ignorant, like all of your kind. Joe didn't force Rob to marry you because it would've been too much of a punishment. He is not too bright, but not even he deserves it."

Alex turned swiftly and tilted her head.

Rob watched, worried, and was surprised by a smirk on her face.

"You are such a bad loser…" the girl said with a cooing tone. She straightened up, lifted her chin and looked at the taller woman with the disdain of a born aristocrat. She flashed her ring in front of Millicent's nose. "Game over, bitch," she spat. "Get the fuck out of our lives."

"You'll pay for this," Millicent said between clenched teeth, opening and closing her hands, ready to pounce. The sparkling diamonds on the ring and the detail in the encasing golden structure revealed a custom-made work by an exquisite artist. And of course, she noticed. Her eyes darted toward Hack again, and they meant business. He'd just been added to her "to hate" list.

Hack nodded to Mr. Renton, his bodyguard, and the military looking man stepped in front of her.

"This way, please," he said, looking at the door curtly and back to her.

"I'm not leaving, and you can't touch me. I'm going to be right over there and there is nothing you can do about it."

* * *

Alex

Alex was edgy after the encounter with Millicent. Rob rubbed her back, but she was having a hard time controlling the tears. The fact that the bitch was still there, glued to her cell phone but not leaving, was utterly frustrating.

"Alejandra, why don't you sing?" Janice came to the rescue.

"Alright." Yes, that would help.

She would prefer to dance actually, but Rob's leg was still not fully recovered. They danced every day as part of his exercise treatment, which had been amazing for bonding. Sometimes, when she was in the zone, she felt they really were one…which made this unresolved business with Millicent the broomstick even nastier. Rob was hers. She was not giving him up. If in America they called them bitches, in Argentina they called angry women mares. Alex was a mare alright, ready to kick Milli the bitch to the moon. Only she couldn't… *sigh.*

Alejandra looked for her friend Csilla and found her eating petit fours while chirping happily with Greg and Sam.

"Hey, girly," Sam said, hugging Alex.

"When did you guys come? I didn't see you."

"Right after Cruella Deville," Greg chimed in and rolled his eyes.

Alejandra chuckled. She was glad the air had cleared between them. They were her best friends in the country after all.

"Do you want to sing?" Csilla asked.

"Yes. I would like to add one song, *Se dice de mi*, dedicated to Cruella. Do you know it?"

"Of course! And then we retake the schedule?"

"That's the plan." Both girls grinned.

Csilla traded the space drums to an accordion, and Alejandra picked up the mic. Taking the stance of Tita Merello, the original singer of the song, she started enumerating all her supposed defects with a smirk playing in her lips and bedroom eyes.

"Se dice de mi… (they say about me)
Se dice que soy chueca, (they say that I'm bow-legged)
Que camino a lo malevo, (that I walk like a gangster)
Que soy fiera y que me muevo (that I'm ugly and that I move)
Con un aire compadrón." (like a bully)

When she moved to the benefits, people were already in her pocket, even when most didn't understand a word of what she said. Then she went to the closing:

"Podrán decir, podrán hablar, (they can say, they can talk)
Y murmurar y rebuznar, (they can murmur and bray)
Mas la fealdad que Dios me dio, (but the ugliness that God gave me)
Mucha mujer me la envidió. (many women envied)
Y no dirán que me engrupí, (and they can't say that I'm haughty)
Porque modesta siempre fui. ('cause I've always been modest)
Yo soy así." (I am this way)

When the final note ended, she received an ovation. Millicent lifted her eyes away from her cell phone and trained them on Alex, spitting fire from their grey depths.

Chapter 19

Alex

Alex couldn't wait for the evening to end. Her feet hurt, her back hurt, even her smile hurt, and of course, the presence of Cruella had spoiled the whole party. They had worked so hard to put this together, and now she couldn't enjoy it. She had a really bad feeling about this night and just wanted to get it over with.

She looked out the door and saw a ghost from her past. It couldn't be. Fermin entered the party as if he owned it and walked right toward her. She was frozen in place by the awkwardness of the situation. His eyes were different, somehow; a self-assurance that was not there before.

"Hola, princesa." He kissed her temple and offered one of his smug smiles.

What to do? Push him, run, scratch the son of the bitch all over. Do something.

Alex looked around, desperate, but Rob was not at sight.

Renton did see her, walked towards them stopping just out of arm's reach, ready to pounce.

With his backup, she gathered her wits.

"What are you doing here?" she asked, purposely speaking in English.

"I came to tell you I forgive your tantrum, and you can come back now."

She gawked, just for a second, and regained control. "I beg your pardon?"

"I do, princess. I forgive you. Let's go now." His hand clamped on hers and she shrieked.

In two seconds flat Renton and two other men she hadn't seen before were on Fermin, taking him out the door. Alejandra followed them, engrossed by morbid curiosity.

Once Renton let go of Fermin, he sprinted away as if flying on the devil's wings. Alejandra didn't have much time to sigh in relief, as an instant later she heard swooshing noises and the three guards fell to the ground.

She ran inside, screaming at the top of her lungs.

"Rob! Hack! Renton's down!"

Both men raced out, and when they reached the door, mayhem exploded.

The windows crashed inward under the feet of men dressed in black. The door was covered by another pair in full armor and more arrived behind them.

"FBI, everybody down," someone yelled.

Alejandra was pushed to the floor and handcuffed. The same happened with almost everyone else.

She was unceremoniously lifted by the arm and taken to a black van. In the process, she saw Hack charging like a bull, with the veins of his neck thick and his eyes red, to be stopped by a stun gun.

Rob was handcuffed on the floor and kicking like a sea turtle out of the water. Millicent had her back toward the wall by the door. With her arms folded and a smirk plastered on her face, she was watching everything with perverse interest.

Rough hands forced her into the van, and she fell to the floor when the vehicle accelerated, burning tires. To her surprise, there was only another person in it: Janice. She was pale like a ghost.

"C'mon girl. Everything will be fine."

She moved her head and seemed to be looking at her from far, far away. "You don't understand… it's Marcos," she murmured and went back to her zombie state.

Alejandra chose to keep her spirits high and hope for the best. That was, until she saw the door opening, two thugs picking them up like sacks of potatoes and carrying them into the cavernous mouth of an Air Force jet.

They were strapped to seats placed in a single row on the side of the plane, looking inward, and left there.

The plane was in the air in less than ten minutes.

Janice's eyes were going in circles, taking everything in. At least she was not in a zombie state anymore.

"Does Marcos have connections with the Air Force?"

"Not that I know of, but I wouldn't be too surprised if he did."

Alejandra lost the sense of time and zoned out. When she woke up there was a soldier sitting right in front of her, looking at her thighs. There was plenty of space between the rows of seats, and he didn't look particularly lecherous. Just normal male appreciation.

He noticed he was being watched and looked at her eyes instead.

Alejandra slanted her face and smirked.

"Those are runner's legs," he mentioned.

"Ballet dancer."

He nodded his head in acknowledgment.

"Want some gum?"

"No, thanks. I need to use the ladies' room. I don't think there is one here?"

"There's a chemical bathroom at the back, but I'm not allowed to let you go. I'm sorry. There's a bucket or the door. I recommend the bucket at this time. The door can be *windy*."

There was a moment of silence after the man unlocked her seatbelt.

"Can you take the handcuffs off me? Leave for a second?"

"I'm sorry I can't do that."

Alejandra looked at the bucket and her dress trying to figure out how to do this in a dignified way.

The soldier slid toward her again, lifted her skirt and removed her panties in a single smooth movement, letting them fall around her ankles.

Alejandra gawked at him, not knowing if she should thank or curse him.

He turned, giving his back to her.

"Just one favor?" he asked.

"Hum?"

"If you're going to attack me, finish the job. I have a young child with special needs. I prefer to leave a good pension than try to take care of him while facing my own disability."

Alex was too worried about her personal situation to understand what the man was talking about. She squatted as best she could, not letting the skirt get into the bucket, and did her business, dying of shame.

"Err I'm done."

The man turned. There was surprise in his good-American-boy face.

"You want them back on or removed?" His chin did a quick jerk and Alejandra knew he was talking about her panties.

She closed her eyes and a single tear fell along her cheek. She had been through a lot since she arrived in the U.S., but never this. For some reason, it reminded her of her oldest brother's patients. That moment when a person needs help for the most intimate things is so sad. Nobody should have to go through it.

She felt a thumb wiping her cheek and opened her eyes to see his sparkling.

"Please don't cry. I can't stand to see a woman crying. I'll put them back, ok?"

She nodded and more silent tears streamed freely down her face.

He bent down, took her panties with two fingers of each hand and pulled them all the way up without touching her skin.

"Please sit down."

She obeyed, and he strapped her to the seat again.

When he came back from clearing the bucket and sat down on his own side, she nodded.

"Thanks for being so kind," she said.

One side of his mouth quirked. "Thanks for not killing me."

She crumbled her face. "Why do you keep saying that? How on earth am I going to kill you?"

His upper torso bent down and his hands racked his short hair.

"You're not really a Russian assassin, are you?"

"A what?" Alejandra's brows shot up wrinkling her forehead.

He shook his head. "I knew it," he murmured.

"Is that what they told you?"

He sighed, his eyes darting to the plane cabin. "Is it there anyone to contact?"

"Hack Humphrey," Janice chimed in for the first time.

"I'll do my best." He nodded once.

Chapter 20

Rob

"So, where are they?" Rob asked for the fifth time, pacing back and forth in Hack's home office like a caged tiger.

"They're over the North of Africa now," he answered. He was crouched in front of the monitor with both hands pulling his hair, following the GPS signals of the women's rings.

"What the hell?"

"I don't know. We'll have to wait for them to land."

"I don't want to wait!"

"Mr. Renton," Hack called.

"Yes, sir." The man lifted his eyes from the computer where he was conducting three chat sessions at the same time.

"News?"

"This is what we know so far: There was an anonymous call to the FBI saying there were Class A substances in Dr. MacArthur's practice disguised as pain killers. Some of the confiscated medicines do contain opiates several times more concentrated than the allowed amount. There will be trouble on that front. My FBI sources still don't know who gave the order to actually attack that day. The whole file is missing. My sources don't know anything about Janice or Alex. Picking them up wasn't part of the FBI operation. ICE has no record of them or a raid in the clinic's location either. Since they're illegal, we can't use any government contacts. Diplomatically they pretty much don't exist."

Rob hit the wall with the side of his fist.

Hack sighed.

"You're not helping, Rob."

"I've never felt so helpless in my whole life."

"We'll find a way... we have to," Hack muttered.

"May I share an observation?" Renton asked. "Why don't you overlap the refuel landing locations and the air force bases? That bird doesn't move like a private jet."

"Of course... how did I not see it before? This is a cherry operation," Hack said.

His hands flew on the keyboard under Rob's stunned eyes.

"Did you just say there was heroin in my pain killers?"

"Unfortunately sir, it's a distinct possibility."

"Millicent..." Rob said with venom in his voice and his fist hit his own hand now. "Hack, are you still listening to the bitch's phones?"

"I'm recording, yes, but I'm behind in processing."

"Let me do it. I need to do something useful before I break your place or myself, whichever comes first."

"Alright. Mr. Renton, please set up another station for Rob with the recordings. Then start pulling your Air Force strings. See if someone saw something. Rob," Hack added, "there's a standing punching bag in the gym. Use it if frustration builds up again."

After about an hour of listening to Millicent's stupid quarrels, Rob was in need of that punching bag. The woman could talk nonstop. Horses and greenery were favorites. "Weird," Rob's mumbled. She'd never looked like an outdoorsy kind of woman.

"Gotcha," Hack said.

Rob lifted his eyes to look into two pools of despair.

"The flight destination is Al Dhafra. They are taking them to the Emirates."

Rob felt his heart sink. "Sharia law?" he asked.

"Yes."

"How strong?"

"Enough…"

"You mean…"

"They're not stoning women for showing their ankles yet, but they can be imprisoned for extramarital sex if they are raped and report it."

"They're being delivered into slavery."

"Pretty much. Yes."

"Hack, this has to be Millicent…"

"There is a bitch-revenge flavor to it, isn't there?"

"I think I'm ready for that punching bag…"

"I'm coming with you. Mr. Renton, adjust the flight plan, please, and start the permission requests."

Hack took the first turn, hitting that bag with passion. Whoever was on the receiving end of those fists would suffer.

Rob went second and it felt really good to let go of his frustration. He kept Millicent's image in his mind while delivering punch after punch. It was an efficient way to unleash his wrath on the deserving bitch's face without going to jail for gender violence.

"Enough," Hack said, grabbing him by the shoulder.

"Now I see how you keep cool. I'm getting one of these." Rob's voice came out in gasps. He could hardly breathe.

"There should be one in any home with men, especially within cities. There would be a lot fewer problems."

"Now what?"

"Bathroom's over there. Take a shower. I'll do the same. Then we go get our ladies back."

Rob kept thinking about Millicent and the heroin while he cleaned up. They had to be related. And now the United Arab Emirates. He was not an expert in international mafias, but he knew about the opium wars of the British Empire and had read the basics of the present development in books like *Dope Inc.* and *Drugs as Weapons Against Us.* Afghanistan was the center of the poppy fields in the East, and there was also a place in Mexico, was it Sinaloa? Something like that. He'd never thought about it much until now.

How the hell did his girl get caught in this mess? And who was the real target? It couldn't be her. There were too many players involved. Him? How? Why? The only thing he did was to practice medicine… Could it be Janice or Hack? *Fuck.*

Chapter 21

Alex

"Please, ladies…" The soldier held two face pieces, one in each hand.

"You want us to use a muzzle? What are we? Dogs?" Alex asked, hands on hips. She was fully dressed in a burka.

The soldier chuckled.

"No, you didn't!" she said, with a straight face but a twinkle in her eyes.

"C'mon, Alex… Leave the poor man alone," Janice chimed in, with a tiny smile and bobbing her head.

"It's called a battoulah. Consider it an improvement. This way you don't need to cover the full face with cloth and can actually breathe."

"What's next? A collar and a leash?"

"I don't know about that." He sobered all of a sudden. "But, trust me, you want to use the whole thing when outside at all times."

"Tell us why," Janice asked, her voice almost a whisper.

"I don't know how to say this…"

"Just go. We can take it," Alejandra encouraged him.

"Well… Essentially if you are seen without full cover, men will assume your legs are open for business. And if you complain you are the one punished. You don't want that…"

"No, we don't," Janice said, her eyes downcast.

They felt the plane changing altitude.

"Please, sit. We're about to land," the soldier said.

"Where are we?" Janice's asked when he was tightening the straps.

"I'm not allowed to provide that information. I'm sorry."

Janice's eyelids closed, her breathing became slow and controlled.

"Abu Dhabi," he murmured in her ear.

The plane took a deep dive and landed. The back opened and a group of six soldiers trotted inside. Alejandra watched, amazed, while a jeep actually entered the fuselage and the soldiers unloaded a pile of packages from the space between the seats. Only to fill in the jeep with other packages, which were piled in the front of the plane.

One of the guys came toward them. He looked like someone you don't want to find in a lonely alley. That man had done some bad things in his life and he owned each one of them.

"Special delivery?" he asked, smirking at the soldier that had been with them all the time. Alejandra wondered what his name was. No time to ask now. He would be just the *good soldier* in her mind.

"Careful," he said. "They're Russian assassins."

The lecherous one snorted. "Sure they are."

He took Alejandra's face and tried to move it to the side.

She bared her teeth and growled.

The man snorted again but let her go.

"These are really pretty. Whites are worth more."

"I can't believe you just said that!" Alex retorted, outraged.

"Don't blame me for the market rules... I like them all colors. It's just a matter of supply and demand."

"They're good girls," the good soldier said.

"Most of the Latin girls are when they first arrive..." the other man answered, showing no hint of humanity in his hard eyes. "Alright," he said, pulling out a stun gun. "Are you going to cooperate and do as you're told, or I start your education right here right now?"

"It depends on what you ask. There are limits that won't be crossed." Janice's voice seemed to come from far away. Her eyes were intense. Alejandra almost didn't recognize her friend. With those clothes and

only her green eyes to see, she looked like a priestess or a shaman…
or a ghost. It was spooky.

The man gave a step back.

"You will be requested to climb the jeep. Then you will be requested
to climb a limo that will take you to your destination."

"To that, we can oblige without forcing you to spoil the merchandise, but not a finger on any of us."

His chin jerked. "Deal."

She nodded in agreement.

Alejandra exchanged eye contact with the *good soldier*. They were
both equally stunned.

"Climb in," the guy said after removing the handcuffs, and both girls
obeyed. It was not easy though. They were not used to the bourkas,
and they stepped on the long cloth more than once before getting it
right.

He climbed to the front seat and drove the jeep off the plane and
into a scorching heat of the Emirates.

The man pulled his phone.

"We have a problem… The new guy, Martin, is not cut out for the
job… No. Don't kill him yet. Something with no lasting effect. Say it
was an accident. Discharge him… Yes. A shrinks' round."

He turned and looked at the girls.

"Whatever hope you put in that guy is gone. He'll be in the hospital for the next couple of weeks and be a zombie when discharged.
If you want to live, accept what's offered, provide what's requested,
and shut the fuck up. If you're sent back, your new destination will
be the Afghan underground bunkers as breeders. Trust me: you don't
want that life."

With downcast eyes, Alejandra's hand went to the child Virgin
Mary pendant, which hung from her neck, seeking protection. Her
hand touched the ring instead, and she gave thanks for the muzzle
that hid her smile.

Chapter 22

Rob

After having a quick shower, Rob found Hack already at his station.

"They stopped moving," he simply said.

"Where are they?"

"Burj Mohammed Bin Rashid."

Rob whistled. "Over ninety floors?"

"Ninety-two," Renton corrected.

"And the satellite only retrieves GPS latitude and longitude. We need more intel or to actually be there to locate them."

"So, when are we leaving?"

"Already on it. This is a transcontinental trip. The flight plan will take time, especially because we need to refuel in different countries, some of them war zones, and we need permits for each one of them."

"We don't have time! At this moment they could be being raped!"

"Don't you think I know that already?" Hack growled. His eyes were in flames.

"Sorry... sorry." Rob took a deep breath and sat at his own station. Something in Millicent's calls was just odd. Maybe focusing on solving the puzzle would keep his murderous thoughts at bay.

Hubert Wilson entered, talking over the phone. He lifted his index finger and all eyes zeroed in him.

"Thank you for your service. I'm putting you in speaker."

"Is Hack Humphrey there?" a male voice Rob didn't know asked.

"Here," Hack replied.

"Two girls. Both with black hair, one with green eyes, one with brown. Both pretty. The one with brown eyes is a ballet dancer. The one with green eyes gave me your name."

"You have them? State your price."

"No. My name is Technical Sergeant Martin Robinson. I was their guard on an Air Force flight to the Emirates. I was told they were Russian assassins who accepted repurposing instead of termination, but they had the chance to kill me and didn't. And then my supervisor said they were Latin."

The man sighed.

"I didn't sign up for this shit. I entered the Air Force to serve my country, not drug cartels and slave traffickers."

"Where are they?"

"I don't know. Somewhere in Abu Dhabi. The guy that took them is Lieutenant Elijah Samir. He surely knows."

"You mentioned drugs?"

"Yes. Poppy gum and hashish eggs go home, pills and cocaine come back with the mail flights. I don't know much more."

"Are you in danger?"

"I just was shot at, but they missed. Whatever happens now, what's done is done."

"Thank you. How can I reward you?"

"If I don't come back, please take care of my wife and child. My son's autistic. This is why I asked for extra duty and got caught in this mess."

"Deal."

"Go to Ras Ghurab Island," Rob chimed in. "Look for Steve at MacArthur Enterprises. Say Rob sent you. You can lie low there for as long as you need."

"Who are you?" the soldier asked.

"Dr. Robert MacArthur, the pretty ballet dancer's guy."

"Alright, bye."

"Thank you. Bye."

"Now what?" Rob asked, as soon as the call ended.

"Sir," Renton interrupted. "There's a patriot's league inside the forces which has been resisting the cherries for years. They could provide assistance to Technical Sergeant Robinson."

"Please proceed," Hack conceded. "Can they help us out?"

"They can keep their eyes open to provide intel, but I'm not sure if they would blow their cover for us..."

"I know. Taking back our country is more important than our girls."

"Sad but true. If they were American..."

"Understood." Hack snarled, his face depleted of any emotion.

Rob looked at his friend and controlled the urge to hide under the table. The last time he saw this expression, mayhem followed.

Hack shook his head, took a couple of deep, shaky breaths and channeled his fury toward the keyboard.

A phone rang, and Rob pulled it out.

It was his father.

"What the hell happened last night?" Joe MacArthur asked rudely.

"Ask Millicent."

"You keep refusing to take responsibility for your own actions? When will you grow up?"

"What the hell are you talking about?"

"You sold drugs to buy the materials for the clinic, didn't you? You know... I didn't want to believe it. But..."

"I did not!" Rob screamed into his phone.

"It's all over the news! You sleazy little wimp!"

"Then it's fake news! You know what? For once I have bigger problems than your bigotry. Millicent sold Alex and Janice to slave traffickers and now they are in Abu Dhabi, probably being raped. So as entertaining as it is to listen to your senile gibberish, I will kindly ask you to *go fuck yourself and leave me the hell alone!*"

Rob cut the phone call and fixed his eyes on the wooden surface of the table, trying to regain his balance and rein back his galloping heart.

The phone rang again, and he threw it toward the wall. Hubert Wilson caught it in midair, showing soccer goal-keeper skills completely out of place for his age. His eyes twinkled with mischief.

"Hello? I'm Hubert Wilson, Mr. Humphrey's head of security... Sorry. He can't. We're in an emergency as you already heard... Yes, sir. It's true... Yes, Janice too... Mr. Humphrey could use your expert assistance in this matter, sir... You have businesses on Ras Ghurab Island?... We need a fast flight to Abu Dhabi that doesn't go through customs. And local support... Perfect. Thank you."

Hubert, still on the floor, panned his audience, smiling.

"What are you waiting for? Get your passport. You're going to the UAE."

"How?"

"Qatar diplomatic jet."

Rob's jaw went slack.

Chapter 23

Alex

"Wow. Look at this view!" Alex exclaimed, looking out the floor to ceiling windows. They had an ocean view that ran for miles.

The lecherous soldier, as Alejandra called him, had been true to his word and taken them all the way to their destination without trying the merchandise. They were in an ample studio, completely painted white, with white porcelanato floors and a wall to wall closet on the side. The bathroom and built-in kitchen were also white. A breakfast bar separated the kitchen area from the completely-bare main floor.

They were on a really high floor, based on how small everything looked in the distance, but she couldn't tell exactly where. As soon as they entered the limo, their heads had been covered with a thick cloth that rendered them completely blind.

Janice came to her side. "No way to escape from here..." she mentioned.

Alejandra nodded, sobering. All of a sudden, the view wasn't so great anymore. There was only one way out from the apartment and the door was locked.

"Maybe a helicopter? I can certainly see H..."

"Shush..." Janice's eyes rolled all the way around their sockets.

Alejandra scanned the room, trying to figure out where the cameras were. She certainly felt observed, now that she thought about it. She realized she was in a creepy version of the Big Brother show. *Great!*

"What do we do now? Change clothes?"

"We can't. We're in someone else's home. Not ours. If we take off the bourka, we breach the local customs and give a green light to our host."

"The muzzle stays too?"

"No. The muzzle definitely goes."

"Thanks be to God!"

Easier said than done; getting rid of the battoulah without removing the headcover and showing their hair was a tough challenge. They chose a very dull, white wall to corner themselves, and used each other's bourkas as a second wall to hide the procedure. It reminded Alejandra of the way they used towels as a tent to change wet clothes at the beach.

After taking the muzzle off, they surveyed their environment. The cabinets had only potato chips and corn snacks, the fridge was stocked with beer and energy drinks, the kitchen and microwave didn't work, there was no cutlery, and only saw plastic plates and cups. The bathroom was working properly, but again, the glass was not real glass.

"I guess they don't want us to have an accident," Alejandra commented.

"Indeed," Janice answered.

Searching the wall to wall closet they found a built-in king-sized bed and a wardrobe containing mostly satin bathrobes, sexy maid Halloween costumes and lacy underwear. Some panels didn't open, and they decided to leave them for the time being.

"Do we dare eat?" Alex asked.

"None of it is food. It's just chemical warfare, very salty chemical warfare."

The girls put the bed back in place, closed all the doors and sat on the floor to wait.

Hours went by and Alex was very thirsty. Hunger was easier to control, but thirst had an urgent element to it that was extremely hard to resist.

"Do you think it's safe to drink water?" he asked Janice.

"No." Janice's voice sounded pasty.

After some more time passed, she couldn't take it anymore and went to the kitchen.

"No!" Janice said. "That's how Marcos got me."

"I've got an idea."

Alex looked into the kitchen cabinets until she found the plastic cups. She took a pile to the bathroom. With determination, she turned on the faucet of the shower and placed the first cup underneath the stream.

Janice was watching unimpressed.

"That's tank water. Even if the feeding water is clean, it could be dead rat and poisonous algae soup."

"I know," answered Alejandra grinning. "Take them to the kitchen."

Janice obliged shaking her head.

After fifteen minutes of work, they had filled the whole pile.

"Here goes nothing," Alejandra said and drank from one of them.

"And the reason is…"

"Shower water might make us sick, but it will not drug us. Not yet anyway, as they are probably trying to correct the mistake as we speak."

"Good thinking. Cheers!" Janice drank as well.

The locked door smacked open and a guy entered dressed in a black robe over white pants and a red checked keffiyeh. He seemed to be in his late twenties or early thirties, and he was fuming with rage. Behind him, there were two goons with shotguns.

Janice moved fast from the kitchen to the living area where he could see her, lifted her tunic a bit to show her feet in a bad first position of ballet, and placed both hands toward the front with her arms bent.

The man stopped in his tracks, watching her with curiosity and a hint of fear.

"I beg your assistance, brother," she said bending down in a small curtsy.

"You are not from the brotherhood," the man said, smirking. "Where did you learn the distress sign? Internet?"

"No," she said placing hands on hips. "I saw my father doing it, only I was too much in shock to take in all the details at the time." She looked at her pose. "What did I miss?"

The man squinted. "Body parts. Who are you?"

"I'm Yanina Suarez," she said uncovering her hair. "Google me," she added, covering her hair again. "My father is Senator Miguel Suarez, a twelfth-degree mason from the chapter of Bogotá, last time we talked about it."

"And your mother?"

"María Adelia Schmitz de Suarez. She is Ruth of the Order of the Eastern Star in the Bogotá chapter. Again, last time we talked about it."

"Schmitz as in Hermann Schmitz?"

"Nazi SS transitioned into Deutsche Bank's Hermann Schmitz? God, I hope not... My grandfather's name was Francisco, or so he said."

The man took a pillow from the closet and sat on the floor.

"And you entered the US illegally to live your life as you pleased without the interference of your parents?" He questioned, smiling, but his eyes were hard.

Janice took a pillow and sat as well, making sure her legs were completely covered.

"Not really. I was the CEO of a small branch of the Bogotá bank in Cartagena when my father managed to send my teen boyfriend in jail using dirty tricks. The man decided to kidnap me as revenge and sent goons after me. I had to flee to the US. In the process, I met my fiancé. Again, just google my name. You will have a good deal of the story."

The man pulled out a cell phone and looked at it for some time, typing, reading and just thumbing the visor. His face paled into a greyish tone as time went by.

"Your teen boyfriend is coca lord Marcos Argüelles?"

"He wasn't a narco when we dated."

"He just published a press release talking about you."

"Really? I haven't seen it." Janice's face crumbled as if waiting for a blow.

"He says he cherished you as his first woman and would never hurt you. He also says that if your present man, Hack Humphrey, doesn't treat you right, he will have a word with him. The same goes for anyone else."

Janice shook her head. "Why did he do it? Why would he embarrass me like that?"

"Maybe he found out you were missing and decided to send a message to... well... me."

The man scratched his thick black beard, "Hack Humphrey? As in Hack-ing anything Humphrey, grandson of CIA founding father Theodore Humphrey?"

Janice shrugged. "I don't know much about his family but could be. He is really good with computers. Owns HH LLC, the online store."

The man took his head between his hands and rocked back and forth. "Allahu Akbar," he whispered a couple of times.

"And you?" he asked Alex. "Don't tell me you are black Venetian royalty."

Alejandra chuckled. "I'm half Italian, half Basque, born in Argentina. No royal blood or funky handshakes in my family that I know of."

"So I can keep you?" his eyes were hopeful.

"Saint Virgin Mary, I hope not..."

The man rolled his eyes and chuckled. "What's your story?"

"I'm a tango dancer. A company hired me with my partner to dance on Broadway. When I arrived in the U.S., the receiving party was a bit too spirited for my liking. A very kind couple helped me escape and I found myself penniless in New York. I could have asked my family for help, but they were against the trip in the first place, so I decided to work and buy the ticket back on my own. In the middle of that, I met Rob, my fiancé, and everything changed."

"And Rob is?"

"Robert MacArthur."

"No secret handshakes in his family?"

"I don't know. His father has money, something about real estate. He is not nice, so he could be into funky stuff. Rob is an MD, like my older brother and father."

"Let me see…" the man said and searched his phone again. "Is the name of your father-in-law Joseph?"

"Yeah," she answered.

"Let me show you something," he said, standing up and walking toward the window.

Alex approached carefully.

"See that island over there?"

"Yes," she answered.

"He owns half of it."

Alejandra shrugged. "Money can't buy happiness. No doubt about it."

He touched her cheek with the back of his hand. "You are very beautiful. Stay with me. I'll make you my pleasure wife instead of my maid."

Alejandra quickly gave a step back and shook her head.

He sighed deeply. "Alright," he said, his index finger scrolling over the screen of his phone.

"Wait!" Janice said.

"What?" His eyes zeroed on her.

"What are you doing?" She questioned.

"I'm just calling the staffing company to say you didn't fit the purpose and ask them to pick you up. I asked for two nice Latin girls to work as maids. You are a completely different ballgame."

Alejandra put hands on hips. "Staffing company? Really? Hmph!"

Janice's eyes went round. "Please don't."

"So now you want to stay? Sorry, I can't have you. You're too dangerous. I could keep her, but only if she wants to stay. Her man's a pussy, but I wouldn't challenge his family."

"Rob's not a pussy!" Alejandra's face went red with anger.

Janice put herself in front of the man.

"If you refuse us, they will send us to the caves in Afghanistan, not back home."

His head slanted. "Sorry, but that's none of my business." He turned on his heels and left, locking the door behind him.

Chapter 24

Rob

The plane made its first refueling stop and Rob stood to exercise his legs. Having his father on the same plane, looking at him all the time, was highly upsetting. It was logical that if the Qatar embassy lent him the plane without reservations, he had to be on board. Yet…

When he arrived at the door, Rob bumped into a heavy-set a man he didn't know. He was surprised, but not as much as to when he heard Hack at his back.

"Marcos Argüelles, what the hell are you doing here?"

"I'm on this flight. What the hell are *you* doing here?"

Turning, he saw Hack fuming. It was almost as if smoke was coming out of his nostrils.

"Enough!" Hack snarled. He was definitely not going to take any bullshit. "How did you know of this flight?"

"I have people in Teterboro."

Hack nodded two times and studied a spot on the carpeted floor for three long breaths. "You did this?" He asked lifting his burning eyes into Marcos' smirking face.

The man sighed. "No… I'm here to help." He shook his head slowly. "You know? I thought that seeing you with your balls tied up would be fun, but it's not. Not when Yani's involved."

More men were entering the plane, some with heavy ammunition. Renton stood between them and Hack, and they stopped, waiting for further instructions.

"Get the hell out of here!" Hack spat.

"Do you know where she is?"

"None of your business."

"Good. Cause I know who has her, but I don't know where."

"You know who has her?"

"Yes. I'll tell you once we are in the air if you let us go with you and help."

"No."

"Man, you are against the cherry U.S. air force AND the Harb brotherhood inserted in the Emirates government. I can negotiate and buy her out. I don't think they will make deals with you."

"No."

"Don't you get it?" The man was losing the cool. "They *will* kill her when they realize she is a liability."

Hack sat.

"What's in it for you?" he asked.

Marcos took the seat in front of him where Rob had been a minute before. "Yani was the best thing that ever happened to me. I fell in love with her when I was five. As you can imagine, this is not easy for me. But in all honesty, I don't see a life worth living if she is not around. Even if she's with you."

Hack shook his head. His eyes fixed on the carpet.

"Something else?"

"Her mother called me to strike a deal. They will give me and my people a general pardon if I help with this, bring her back safely… and quit."

"Are you ready to quit?"

"Of course. They also let me keep my assets, *on the white.*"

Wow.

"Just a sec…" Hack said. He pulled his phone, plugged the earbud and speed-dialed a number.

"Who are you calling?"

"Janice's mom..."

Marcos sighed and stretched his legs.

"Hi... Yes, she's been kidnapped... Did you call Marcos?... Yes, he's here. Do you trust him?"

Hack's eyes squinted as Maria Adelia talked and information sank in. Finally, he closed the call and looked at Marcos squarely:

"If you double-cross me..."

"I won't," the man answered.

Hack nodded his head to Renton. Renton moved out of the way and half a dozen men silently entered the plane, carrying heavy sports bags.

"Mackey, the door," Renton said.

The man secured the door with military precision.

Renton disappeared into the cabin and soon Rob heard the pilot in the speakers. "Please, find a seat and fasten your seatbelts. We're leaving in five minutes."

Rob had watched the whole situation unfold with fascination. *What's just happened?*

"Spit it out!" Hack said once they were up in the sky.

Marcos retrieved a manila folder. Rob wondered why they always had to be manila folders. And who started the trend? Was it the bad guys slash spies or Hollywood? *Focus.*

In the folder, there was a picture of a man dressed up in full Arab gear.

"Tashif Al Cassar. He trades weapons and MREs from U.S., stock to the different factions of the brotherhood.

"He has properties all over the world, from Siberia to Patagonia. I wouldn't be surprised if he had bought a parcel on Mars as well."

The man noticed Rob's smirk, and he laughed without humor.

"Yes, they are selling parcels in Mars. They offered me one, right in the Scientology neighborhood. Lots of celebrities. Do you see *me* there? Please..."

Rob snorted and Marcos smirked.

Marcos looked at Hack, sobering.

"Your turn."

"I never said I would share information," Hack answered sternly, and Rob could swear his lower lip came out in a pout.

"Is he always this unnerving?" Marcos asked Rob.

"Not really. I think trying to steal his woman and drug her didn't put you on his best buddies' list. I would probably be at your throat right now, damn the consequences, if it had been Alex."

"Fair enough. Who's Alex? The other girl?"

"Yeah," Rob pulled his phone and showed him a video of Alejandra performing at the clinic inauguration.

While Marcos watched, Hack went to the furthest corner of the plane, pulled out his computer and satellite phone, hooked them into the sockets to the external antenna and started stroking keys as if his life depended on it.

The man's eyes drifted toward Hack, and Rob had a glimpse of how fast and dangerous he really was.

"Look. I will do my best to entertain you for the rest of the flight, while Hack does his magic. And you will stay with me and keep on pretending you care about Janice. Get it?"

Marcos' eyes burned into his for a second, then nodded. "I do care. And her name is Yanina."

Chapter 25

Alex

"Asshole!" Alex yelled at the closing door and threw one of her stilettos at it. The shoe made a satisfying *thump*, before falling to the floor.

Janice watched her, her lips twisted in a smirk.

"What? It feels good. You try!" Alejandra challenged.

"Alright," Janice said and took her own shoe off, went toward the door and scratched the wood with its heel, writing the word "Asshole".

The heels of both girls' shoes had metal points instead of plastic, so they were sharp as needles.

Alejandra crossed her arms in front of her body and watched the other lady's job appreciatively. "Oh, I like that…"

She picked up her own shoe and wrote: "Fucking son of a bitch" and signed with a flowery "Alejandra" right under it.

"You forgot to sign," she said to Janice.

"You are right…" the other girl said, and wrote her own name, both in English and Hispanic versions. She looked at it, slanting her head and added her last name, and both her parents' names to the Spanish one.

"Now what?"

"I've got an idea," Alejandra said, looking at the closet.

She opened all the doors she could and pulled everything out, making mayhem on the pristine white floor.

"That's just silly."

"I know. Help me."

Janice shook her head but obliged.

Alejandra walked around spreading the mess as much as possible.

"Oh, these are pretty," she murmured picking up a pair of silk Japanese kimonos. She caressed the soft fabric between her fingers in awe, brought it to her lips and kissed it. "I'm sorry..." she said before heading with the robes to the bathroom.

"What are you doing?" Janice asked, evidently worried.

"Shower," Alejandra simply said.

Once in the bathroom, she turned on the water and put the kimonos on the tub, blocking the drain.

"Oh," Janice said. She disappeared into the main floor and came back with a handful of skimpy, open-crotch panties. She threw one at a time in the toilet and pressed the button.

"Ok, that's just nasty. What if we need to go?"

"We'll manage," Janice answered. "This will hopefully block more than one floor, and people will come asking questions."

"What now?"

"I don't know... chemical warfare?"

"That could work. You stay here and keep working the toilet."

Alejandra went to the main floor. What had started as just blowing off steam had morphed into leaving a mark they were here for Hack and Rob, and now she was determined to create as much damage as possible before leaving.

If they only could buy some time, she was sure their men would find them. At least they had to try and keep trying. What else could they do?

Alejandra looked at the mess in the living area. If they just could barricade themselves.

Her initial idea coming to the living room was to open all the packages of pseudo food and get everything dirty. But now she had other plans. They might need to eat, after all.

She went into a frenzy, piling the clothes toward the door and pushing them under it with the heels of the shoes. Once she was reasonably satisfied, she picked up the shoes and set them on the breakfast bar. Funny enough, those were the closest to weapons they had.

She saw with satisfaction how the water was crawling its way into the living room. Soon it would reach the other apartment, the one behind the door. For a second, she feared the clothes would create a deadly pool. But soon she realized it wasn't happening. The door would be harder to open though. Good.

Janice came into the room and saw her work. "Oh…" she said. "We need something bigger."

"Any ideas?"

"The fridge?"

"Let's try."

The fridge was friggin heavy. They had to remove everything—mostly beer and energy drink cans—from the inside to be able to slide it off the kitchen furniture.

They'd managed to get it almost to the door when they heard the lock.

With a desperate war cry, Alex pushed the fridge the last three feet and smacked it toward the already opening door.

She heard a grunt and kept pushing until the door was closed again. Janice was already running to the kitchen area to get the racks and cans back. Alejandra rested her back on the fridge and looked at her.

Janice was frozen in place, her eyes locked on the window and her arms filled with cans. On the other side of the tall glass, there was a man hanging from a cable with climbing gear, all dressed in black, and cutting a small circle in the crystal. Hope spread into Alex's heart.

He removed his goggles and smiled at the girls ferally. It was the *bad soldier*. He threw a can inside the broken glass and smoke filled the air.

"Get the shoes," she yelled and ran to put her shoes on. Janice did the same and they both passed out holding hands on the soaked floor by the breakfast bar.

Chapter 26

Rob

It was a bright day in Abu Dhabi, as it normally was most of the year. The rental van arrived literally to the plane's door, and both Renton's and Marco's men got right to work. Rob found it very interesting. They could cooperate with zero animosity right now and kill each other the next minute depending on their orders.

He also found it interesting how they could move so much ammunition through customs completely unchecked. In normal flights, he had to even take his shoes off and accept being cooked in a microwave oven—or let a total stranger get comfy with his privates. Here, real bad guys moved with total impunity. *Something is wrong with this picture.*

"Who's driving?" Hack asked.

"Ali is our guy in the city," Marcos answered. "He knows every place and every person that's worth knowing."

"Get the hell out of there!" Hack told the man.

Marcos placed himself in front of Hack, their chests almost touching. Hack was taller, but Marcos didn't seem a bit intimidated.

"We don't have time for more bullshit," Marcos said carefully.

"Mr. Renton," Hack called. His men stood alert.

"Yes, sir."

"Recommendations?"

"Time is sensitive, so my recommendation is to use the local guide. My people already have his personal information. In case of unsatisfactory performance, due diligence will be taken."

The man swallowed.

"Alright, let's go," Marcos said, opening the door.

"Mr. Renton, take the front seat," Hack said.

Marcos quirked the side of his mouth.

Hack took a seat and opened his computer again.

"So, where to?" Marcos asked with a hint of exasperation.

"Holy shit! They're moving again!"

They followed the signal to the E20, a fairly good road and then the E75 going northeast and into the desert.

"This is not good," the driver said. "The E75 is a truck road and we are heading to the middle of nowhere, at the brotherhood's mercy."

"Don't worry," Marcos said. "I have enough Captagon pills to buy our way out of any trouble."

"In that case, let's hope your God protects us because Allah won't. He doesn't approve of it."

Marcos snorted.

"What's Captagon?" Rob asked.

"Courage in a pill, without the drawbacks of a consciousness. Very addictive. Ideal to train guerrillas and suicide bombers."

"Really?"

"Hell yeah…"

"Hell indeed…" Rob's father murmured.

Rob looked at him, dumbfounded. He had forgotten the old man was around.

"We have a problem," Hack interjected.

"You mean another one?" Marcos asked.

"The signals separate. They're taking them to different places."

"Do you know who's who?" Marcos asked.

"Unfortunately, no. I made both rings for Janice. Giving one of them to Alex was an afterthought. They both have the same signal."

"Shit, man…"

"So weird. There's no road at the splitting point. Just desert." Hack raked his hair.

"Do the ones in the desert move fast or slow?" asked the driver.

"Slow," Hack answered.

"Bedouins," the man said.

"They probably sold only one there and they are taking the other to the market." Marcos looked nervously out the window.

"Market?" Rob asked.

"Don't ask," Marcos answered, his face blanched and his eyes glued to his cell phone.

Chapter 27

Alex

Alex woke up under a quilt. It was soft to the touch and striped. She lay on another quilt. Her hand went to her neck and the chain with the ring was gone.

"Shit," she whispered.

Her hand opened the covering quilt and she realized she was completely naked.

"Perfect," she heard.

Her eyes shot towards the voice and her hand quickly retrieved the cover. The *bad soldier* was sitting on a rug, with his legs crossed and a cell phone in his hand.

"Did you just take a picture of me?" Alejandra demanded, fuming.

"A really good one. It's ok when they're out cold, but you, opening the quilt and showing the goods... that was priceless."

"You. You. You... conchudo hijo de re mil putas!"

The man snorted.

"Wow, girl. You have a way with words..." He grinned.

Her eyes rounded.

"Do you speak Spanish?"

"Not much, but *coño* and *puta* any soldier knows." His lips quirked.

Alex sighed. "Where are my clothes?"

"Somewhere in the middle of the desert. I sold them to a group of Bedouins."

"You didn't have the right to do it," Janice interjected.

The man moved fast and put himself nose to nose with her. She squeaked and backed up toward the cloth wall of the tent. He took the quilt off her body and shot a photo of her scared face and naked upper torso.

"You're in my world now, sweetheart, and in my world, I have the right to do whatever the hell I want unless someone stops me," he spat the words in her face. "It's a jungle out here. Supremacy of the fittest in its most gory glory." His eyes shone with craziness, really dangerous craziness.

"I'm so going to enjoy the show when Marcos plays soccer with your head," Janice carefully intoned, filling her words with venom.

He grabbed her by the hair and exposed her neck. "That's only if you're alive to see it. Can he stop me now from biting out your larynx? I can fuck that hole while you die. It would take deep throating to a whole new level."

"Be my guest..." she answered levelly.

Only then did Alex fully understood that they were at the end of their rope and Yani was trying to go down with dignity. She felt like they were in the final scene of Thelma and Louis when they jumped with the car into the canyon. Was this really the end? Was she ready to die?

Yani wanted to die before being raped. Alex disagreed though. If they could hang around some more, Alejandra felt they owed it to their men to do their best. Was there life after rape? Probably yes. Would their men still want them? She didn't know. A Latin guy might not. Hack, she wasn't sure. But Rob would sob with her all the way and try to make it better... *I really love him...*

She stood tall in all her naked glory. "Hey! You wanted a nice shot?" she said putting fists on hips, the quilt hanging from her right hand.

The man looked at her, his smile becoming feral.

She took the quilt and covered her lower half. Then her left leg bent and lifted slowly only to extend theatrically into a vertical split. That position drove Rob crazy.

The man stood, forgetting Janice and took a picture.

"Woman, you are full of promise," he said approaching slowly.

She let the leg down and nervously wrapped the quilt around her waist.

He took another picture.

"Not bothering to cover the tits?"

She looked at her chest and made a *tsk* sound. "Nah, I don't mind being topless."

His hand approached her chest tentatively and she swatted it away, taking a step back.

He smirked.

Janice sprinted toward the opening of the tent. The man saw it by the corner of his eye.

"Shit, woman!" he blurted.

Alejandra threw the quilt over his head and ran toward the exit too.

"Seriously?" the man laughed, taking the quilt off his eyes. He shook his head and went after them.

What Alejandra saw on the other side of the tent, looked like the set of a class B dystopian movie. Row after row of cages with naked people inside under another huge tent. Women and children of different shapes and colors caged like animals. There was a bottle of water in one corner, and a plastic bowl with dog food in another. The smells and noises were sickening, and Alejandra felt lightheaded and was about to faint when strong arms picked her up and put her inside one of the cages. Janice was in one by her side in a fetal position, sobbing.

"See?" The bad soldier folded his arms in front of his broad chest and snickered. "I tried to be nice to you and you didn't let me. Now it's beyond my control. Good luck in your new life, wherever it takes you."

"I hope you fry in hell!" Janice said through gritted teeth, and Alejandra realized she was in pain.

"According to your religion, I won't. I just went to the Vatican last month and climbed the Santa Scala on my knees. It grants me instant forgiveness of all my sins for ninety days. That means I have two more months to do whatever I want before having to do it again."

"Do you believe that shit?" Alex asked, bewildered. That couldn't be true, could it?

"I don't, but I do it anyway. It's your religion's shit after all, just like miracles. I'd start praying for one if I were you."

He took yet another picture, turned his back to them and left.

Alejandra looked around her as dismay started to crawl under her skin. She felt like curling up in a ball herself and crying her life away, only that she couldn't. Yani needed help.

"What's going on? Are you hurt?"

"I swallowed the ring. Not a healthy idea."

"Oh, Lord…"

"Don't worry. I'll be alright," Janice said.

The ring.

"That means…"

Janice nodded and closed her eyes.

Alejandra felt warmth spreading in her chest in a way she always identified with Jesus by her side.

There you have your miracle.

Indeed.

Chapter 28

Rob

The desert extended unendingly, like an ocean made of sand, and dust, and death. Rob sheltered his eyes with his hand and looked into the distance, taking in the immensity of its desolation. They had stopped to stretch their legs and to have a closer look at the unique picture displayed in front of them. Right there, interrupting the endless black stripe of the freeway, there were two camels having sex.

"In the middle of the road? Seriously?" Rob asked dumbfounded.

"Well, they happened to be in this area way before the road," the driver said, biting a small stick of cinnamon.

"And there's less sand right here. That's important," Renton spoke for the first time in the two hours' drive.

"Indeed…" the man nodded slowly a couple of times.

"The fork is just a couple of miles ahead," Hack said, always single-minded and not a bit impressed by the scene.

"The helicopter is coming," Renton answered.

"I'll take the helicopter and you follow the road," Marcos interjected. His eyes were bloodshot, and his face depleted of color.

Hack walked with long strides and put himself in front of the man, too close for comfort. "What do you know that I don't?"

"You are invading my personal space," Marcos answered levelly.

"Spit it out!"

"Or what?"

"C'mon. Leave your inner children behind for a second. The girls need us," Rob squeezed between the two men and separated them.

"They made it to the dark web," Marcos said and gave his cell phone to Rob.

Right in front of his eyes, there were pictures of Alex and Janice, naked. Alex had bedroom eyes and was opening a quilt. Janice was completely scared. There was a list of physical characteristics beside the photo, as if they were products. There were more pictures above and below, depicting other victims. The thing looked like a catalog.

Hack took the phone from his hand and sighed noisily. "They're alive."

"And they don't seem roughed up yet," Marcos added and looked at Hack. "But it's an on-site auction."

"Meaning?" Rob asked.

"We need to be there to get them."

"Address?" Hack asked, scratching his neck.

"Of course not… but if you look at the background, they are in a Bedouin tent. The same Bedouin tent I might add."

"And that's why you wanted the helicopter…"

"Well, it's a numbers game. The one in the helicopter can go to both locations, the one in the van can't."

"I'll take it," Hack said through clenched teeth and looking at Marcos defiantly.

"Alright," Marcos said, lifting his hands. "Before you leave, how much do you have in bitcoins for instant transfer?"

"A couple thousand. It's a Ponzi scheme," Hack answered, a shadow of confusion crossing his face.

"Not good enough," Marcos said. "How much do you have?" he asked Rob now.

"Me?" asked Rob. He didn't have any money. Not a red cent except for his collection. How much could he sell it for? He never went through with the appraisal, so he didn't know. Even if he had a number

for it, it wouldn't be enough. He needed bitcoins for instant transfer...
God.

"Twenty-two million. Bid it all, I don't mind. Put half on each girl, whatever it takes," Rob's father interjected.

"Dad?" Rob looked at him with big round eyes.

"What?" Joe answered.

Hack threw himself at the man and hugged him. "Thanks, Joe, I'll pay you back," he said, his face red by the sheer effort of not crying.

"I know, son... I'll transfer the crypto keys to Renton's computer" the old man said, patting his back, and giving Rob a hard look from over Hack's shoulder.

"I'll pay you back too," Rob said with a small voice.

"Sure you will," the old man answered, his eyes hard and small, and his lips stretched.

"Alright, I have another two million, but, sorry, man, they go all to Yani," Marcos said looking at Rob.

Rob nodded.

"Let's start the bidding with two thousand," Marcos said while hitting the glass of his tablet.

"Two thousand?" Hack asked, dumbfounded. "Only two thousand?"

Marcos huffed and kept working. "How many slaves have you bought?"

"None!" answered Hack, outraged.

"Then don't bug me," Marcos said nonchalantly.

"I'm gonna..." Hack started but was restraint by Joe's big paw.

"Let him work, Hack. That's how a normal auction goes. If you bid the maximum to start with, they'll take them off the auction and maybe kill them."

Rob looked at his father. He realized that the man he thought was his father and this man were completely different animals.

"Dad?"

"What?" The old man grunted.

"Do you buy slaves?"

"Yes, I do," he said, nodding slowly and understanding perfectly the effect of the implications. Uncomfortable, he folded his arms in front of his chest.

Rob was outraged, and then he remembered the pictures of himself in the demonstration, and how easy it was to misunderstand things, taking them out of context. His dad was a lot of things, but he was not a monster.

"Someone else doubled. Let's double two," Marcos said and added an eight thousand bet on each girl.

"You use slave labor?" Rob zeroed in his father again.

"Only in this part of the world," he said.

"I can't believe it..." Rob muttered. "Please, Dad, fix this..." he pleaded. "Tell me more, and fix this..."

Rob cried easily and it never bothered him, didn't bother this time either. His father used to hate to see him cry. It wasn't manly enough. This time, he looked up, sighed, and looked at his son again. His eyes also wet.

"People around here are not workers, they are warriors and merchants. They have been for over a thousand years. They consider manual labor a lowly job beneath them as real men, and so they are impossible to work with, especially if you are an *infidel*. They have also been trading slaves for thousands of years; the slave trade never stopped in this part of the world. So, yes, I buy slaves in these markets, free them and offer them work. They are the hardest, most efficient workers I've ever had. Especially Africans. Unbelievable strength and resiliency. They are also fast at learning new skills. When the job is finished, they leave with their pockets full and usually use the money to pay their way into Europe."

Rob sighed, relieved. This was bad but not nearly as bad as he initially thought. He realized he had done right to leave the family business. He didn't have, nor did he want to have, what it took to manage a transnational corporation. This level of pragmatism was beyond his ability to cope.

He also realized something else... it *was* time to man up, because this shady money had supported his comfortable lifestyle, and now was buying his woman's freedom. On his own, he would have lost her.

"Doubled again," Marcos said. "Let's do it," he added, and he changed his bid to thirty-two thousand.

"Bird's here," Renton said, with his hand again over the Bluetooth.

"Where is the noise?" Rob asked, looking around him.

"It's a new model. The tail rotor is encased, so there's almost no noise," Renton explained.

"Rob, are you coming?" Hack asked.

"I think I'm going in the van. I have a hunch."

"Good. You can keep an eye on him..."

Marcos grinned, showing a mile of teeth, and Rob snorted.

"Mr. Renton, you go with them as well, as you have the keys. Split the team. Both signals are stationary, so we have directions."

Renton studied the map. "I would say about forty miles."

"Alright. Let's do this," Hack said.

Renton nodded to his henchman. Mackey nodded back.

Marcos nodded to one of his men, and he nodded back. The man had a scar on his neck from ear to ear and a long tattoo of the Santa Muerte on the inside of his forearm. He'd evidently seen death up close.

Hack went to the van and retrieved two handbags.

Meanwhile, the helicopter had landed. Mackey and two of Hack's other men were already climbing in, followed by tattoo guy and another of Marcos's goons.

Once Hack was safely on board, the blades cut the air and the machine flew.

"C'mon, man, let's get going," Marcos palmed Rob's shoulder amicably and took position in the copilot seat in the front of the van. Renton quirked the right side of his mouth and climbed in the back.

Chapter 29

Alex

"Who are you," the man demanded in perfect English. His long beard was almost to his stomach and hung in front of two manicured hands interlaced over the prominent hump.

That's what Alex first saw. Those perfect, oiled nails and soft hands over a huge belly, with oiled, combed hair hanging in a pointy tail in front of them. It was a display a luxury that made a stark contrast with the cages, and the smell, and her nakedness. Her nails were manicured too, a deep red. She had matched it to her lipstick for Rob's party. The whole situation had a distinctive oneiric patina as if it were one of her bizarre repeated dreams of being naked in different situations. Only it wasn't a dream, was it?

"I'm Alejandra De Luca, and you are?" she asked, standing.

Acting nonchalant being naked in public and especially in front of this man was not something her normal self could manage. It had been different inside the tent. *Why? I don't know.* The bad soldier felt more like a character than a person, and Janice was in danger. But here? *How to solve this? An acting gig… yes, a gig.* Her first acting offer out of school had been a play called Anatomy Lesson, where all the actors were naked on stage. Her family had objected and that was the end of it. Funnily enough, she had her second chance now… She called the actress and cloaked herself in its persona. This wasn't her life. It was an acting gig, and soon it would be over.

"Your future master," the man said, slanting his head and giving her an appreciative once over.

Two rules, said Greg the first day working in the cleaning crew. *No matter what, always be nice and do the work.*

Alex controlled her face and bit her tongue. The smirk and snotty response that were dying to jump from her lips had to be restrained at all costs. Ridiculous as it sounded, their lives depended on it. Her mind slid deeper into the zone. This was an acting gig and she needed to cloak herself in the right fictional character, one designed to keep them safe for the longest time possible. Her mind quickly searched for a reference and she remembered Isabel Sarli. Dressing in the innocent diva style of her younger years would work, but Isabel was too different from her to pull it off right. A touch of Nacha Guevara would add some spice.

She crossed a leg in front of the other and made a deep courtesy as they did at the end of a ballet presentation, purposely ignoring the view she was giving to whoever happened to be at her back.

The man chuckled.

"I was told you would be good for video. Now I see why. Yes, I will make you a movie star," the man said.

Her head snapped up and her nostrils flared as fear took her over for a second. She'd escaped the other bastards to fall in the hands of this jerk? *It's just a gig. Get into character.*

"Do you really want to share all this…" her hands waved around her body, showcasing her assets, "with others?"

He assessed the situation for ten long breaths. "We'll see… It all depends on how nice you are to me. Tell me, how nice are you willing to be?"

"Well…" she cloaked herself in her character even tighter. It felt good; powerful and sensual in a very feminine way, and she managed to project it onto him. "You know how it goes… it depends on how well you treat *me*. I'm unique, and beautiful, and can be *thankful* with the right *incentive…*" She waved her body to one side and the other at the rhythm of her words, and she could see lust shining in the dark pits that were the man's eyes. She didn't have Isabel's lips, nor her boobs, but she could take her enchantress stance and replicate her candid gaze while keeping Nacha's snappy sense of humor.

"And your friend? Is she willing to be nice too?" he moved his chin toward Janice who was curled up into a ball and had managed to almost cover herself in hay.

"Well, if you treat her right too, I will be *very* thankful," she said.

"Tell me something, have you been *very thankful* to someone lately?" The man asked after looking at his phone and typing something.

"Why? Jealous already?" Alex felt part of her façade melting. Something about the phone, and the writing… The guy was frustrated. Could it be Rob and Hack?

"Someone is bidding stubbornly on both of you… tell me, how much are you worth?"

Stay in character. She offered him a coquette smile. "The sky is the limit…"

The man made a tsk sound with his lips, gave her another once over and left.

Her legs failed and Alex fell onto the hay, only to see Janice's deep gaze.

"Hang on," she told her friend, "they're coming."

Janice nodded and hugged her stomach even tighter as she rocked herself.

Chapter 30

Rob

"Barricade," the driver said and pushed the brake, bringing the van to a halt.

"I'll try to buy our way in," Marcos said, twisting his body to see Renton. "If I go down, kill them all and hit the gas."

Both Renton and the driver nodded.

"You two, stay down," he said to Rob and Joe.

"You two, stay or follow me. I leave it to you," he said to his men.

Both nodded.

"I'm coming."

"Me too."

"It's Russian roulette. If they're high, we're dead," Marcos clarified to his men, so they understood the situation.

Both nodded again. One crossed himself, and the other touched the tattoo in the middle of his chest and kissed his bent index finger.

"Let's do this," Marcos said and took a bag from the van's floor.

"I'd like to go," Rob said.

"What for?"

"It makes sense that a white asshole would try to get to the auction, is it not?"

"So you're the white asshole and I'm your brown caddy?"

"Yes. I can play a white asshole anytime, and if they kill us, there's more firepower to go on."

"That makes sense… but here we are in brown land, so maybe I can be the brown asshole and you the white caddy."

"You are an outstanding brown asshole. Let's do it." Rob grinned from ear to ear.

Marcos snorted.

"Let's do it, man."

"I'm going too," Joe said, taking them by surprise.

"And you're coming because?"

"I speak the language…"

Marcos shrugged and opened the door.

With all the weapons trained on them, the three men approached the truck slowly: Marcos in the middle and toward the front. Rob and his father framing him. Rob carried the bag and they all had Google glasses on, showing Renton—and Hack—everything they saw.

"Look to your left, and slowly to your right, once you get to target," Renton's instructions came clear through the Bluetooth earbud.

"Allahu Akbar," Marcos said once they were in front of the convoy. There were four bearded men and one who wasn't. That one caught Rob's eye. *Military.*

"Road's closed. Turn around," the non-bearded man said.

"We are going to the auction. I've got a lot invested already," Marcos answered.

"I know that, Marcos Angüelles. Which of the girls are you here for? The petite spooky one or the hot dancer?"

"Both," he said. "I'm bidding on them to gain them squarely. Trouble only comes if we don't get our girls back."

"What's your highest bid?"

"Who are you?"

"I represent their current owner."

"Two million each, instant transfer by bitcoin, and I can add a commission of two million for you. Instant traffic into your account."

The man chuckled.

"I don't like bitcoins. I want gold."

"I have only fifty grand in gold on me, and probably you could trade the Captagon I carry for a good amount too."

"Captagon? You came loaded…"

"You have no idea, my friend…" Marcos said and took his glasses off, making them go around to show Renton the whole situation.

"Are those Google glasses?"

"They are."

"You think you've got this covered?"

"The girls are covered for good or bad. You and I, on the other hand… are disposable, unless we do something about it."

"Are they disposable too?" he asked, looking at father and son. "Joseph Mac Arthur… he's worth something," the man added. "His puny son on the other hand… is just a leech. Tell me, old man, would you pay anything in ransom or just be happy if my friends here got rid of him?"

Rob could see how the vein on the neck of his father started to thicken, and his face turned red, but he didn't answer.

"You're not getting me," Rob said. "Not alive anyway…"

"Is that a challenge? I love challenges…" the man squinted his eyes and a glimpse of madness peeked from behind his composure.

"Not really, just a fact. Mr. Renton," he said touching his ear. "Kill me if they get me."

"Understood," came the answer.

The man tilted his head.

"How many snipers do you have?" he asked.

"I don't know. Do you want to talk with our tech man?"

"Yes, please…"

Rob took a Bluetooth from his pocket and handed it to the man. He smiled and placed it in his ear.

"Is the van armored, Mr. Renton?"

"There are remote control guns, computer-managed, tracking each hostile target. We also have your outpost within missile range," came from the Bluetooth.

"That would kill the girls."

"That's the only reason you're still alive. To negotiate. If negotiation fails, then everything fails. We bring the girls back. Alive if possible. In pieces, if they're already dead. But we bring them back."

"What will your boss say to this?"

"I'm Hack Humphrey, you asshole. I've already recovered the jewelry from the Bedouins and am now at 10,000 feet looking down on you all.

So the girls are here. Rob felt a surge of excitement.

They could see the tents on the distance, and a series of cars, vans and big trucks parked close by. Rob's shoulders dropped. They would need an army to get in there... or an intelligent bastard who valued his life.

"I'll let you in, but you transfer the full six million to me," he said.

"Can do. We already won the bid for a total of eleven million. so you can have an additional six," Hack said.

"We got them?" Rob asked excitedly.

"Yes," Hack clipped. "Well, what's it gonna be? You want to come out of here rich? Or dead?"

As if on cue, a small red dot appeared in the middle of each man's chest.

The man looked down and into Rob's eyes. "I take rich," he said.

"Take your cell phone and place the bitcoin address in it. Then hand it to Rob so he can transmit your message to me."

"No way in hell I use my cell phone," he said.

"Then use this one," Rob said and handed the man his. "Speed dial one."

The man typed a code into the phone and sent it. Then he took a handkerchief and cleaned it from fingertips before delivering back to Rob.

Hack snickered. "Don't worry, Elijah, we got you covered."

The man blanched.

What came next happened so fast that Rob didn't register it. The man grabbed him by the ear and pulled. Rob felt how his body followed the man's instructions with no resistance, bypassing his own will. It was highly embarrassing. He didn't know you could lead someone like that just by the ear.

The gunfire started and was finished in a few seconds, leaving Rob facing the van, grabbed by his larynx and with a red dot on his chest.

Renton nodded at Rob, and he nodded back. Everybody in the van seemed to be fine. From the corner of his eye, Rob noticed something else. All of the bearded guys in the truck were dead on the ground.

The red dot moved slowly from Rob's chest until it placed itself over the man's nose.

"What's it gonna be?" Hack asked.

"Why didn't you kill me?" the man asked.

"We made a deal, and I already paid you. I expect you to do your part of the bargain and take us in."

"And then?"

"None of my business. My suggestion is that you buy a plot on Mars and move permanently. I'm just retrieving what I bought, but you... will be hunted down by your own side."

Rob felt the pressure on his neck ease, and then he was free.

"Take their clothes," Elijah said nodding his head toward his now deceased companions.

Chapter 31

Alex

The boy couldn't be older than twelve. He put the bowl of dog food in a corner and looked at Alejandra with scorn. He showed the water and said something in Arabic.

"Sorry, I don't understand," she answered in English.

He lifted his tunic and showed his member, small but erect, with hairless testicles. Then he pointed at the water and pumped his member with his fist.

Alejandra was too confused to register what he wanted. The scene was just too bizarre.

"He wants a blowjob in exchange for the water," the same guy that had visited her before said, coming behind the boy.

"Oh. Well, unfortunately, I've just run out. How about a song?"

The man laughed. He certainly enjoyed a good barter. He took the water from the boy's hand and smacked him in the head with it when the kid resisted. The boy ran away. The man looked at Alejandra with hawk's eyes.

"What are you doing here? You're too old."

"Well, thank you," Alejandra answered, standing up and putting hands on hips.

The man smiled again, but his eyes were hard like sapphires.

"Sing," he said, showing the water to her.

Alejandra was definitely thirsty and singing while thirsty was a problem. But a song was a lot more than a song in certain moments. It was a magical incantation. She just knew what to sing.

"Negra, ayudame," she murmured a call for help to Mercedes Sosa, the woman who'd made this song famous all over the world. She started singing.

"Solo le pido a Dios" *(I only ask of God)*
"Que el dolor no me sea indiferente," *(That I'm not indifferent to pain,)*
"Que la reseca muerte no me encuentre," *(That the dry death won't find me)*
"Vacío y solo sin haber hecho lo suficiente." *(Empty and alone, without having done enough.)*

Alejandra felt her voice had a strength that was not hers. It was as if *la Negra* were with her. The man she was singing for looked struck by lightning. "Shā'ir," he murmured.

When she started the second strophe another voice joined her. It was Yani.

"Sólo le pido a Dios" *(I only ask of God)*
"Que lo injusto no me sea indiferente," *(That I'm not indifferent to injustice,)*
"Que no me abofeteen la otra mejilla," *(That they don't slap my other cheek,)*
"Después que una garra me arañó esta suerte." *(After a claw scratched my luck.)*

The duet blended beautifully, and more people began paying attention. When the third verse started, many other voices joined them.

"Sólo le pido a Dios" *(I only ask of God)*
"Que la guerra no me sea indiferente," *(That I'm not indifferent to war,)*
"Es un monstruo grande y pisa fuerte" *(It's a big monster that stomps on)*
"Toda la pobre inocencia de la gente." *(the people's trustful innocence)*

The last two verses repeated once, and she didn't know how to proceed from there. The power in the place was raising, but the song called for an interlude on harmonica.

Then she heard it; the sound came from her right, and when she looked, Rob was there, dressed like a local and playing the tune as if he were Leon Gieco himself.

Alejandra sobbed and choked, but the intensity in his eyes told her it was imperative to keep singing. So she did.

She straightened up and noticed other women standing, ready to join in.

When the interlude finished, she moved to the following verse.

"Sólo le pido a Dios" (I only ask of God)
"Que el engaño no me sea indiferente," (That I'm not indifferent to deceit,)
"Si un traidor puede más que unos cuantos," (If a traitor can do more than many people,)
"Que esos cuantos no lo olviden fácilmente." (Don't let those people forget him easily.)

The man in front of Alex was now watching Rob fixedly. He took a dagger out of his clothes and moved to attack him. He didn't get far though. Renton appeared out of nowhere, pulled the man's hair up, exposing his neck, and buried his knife through to the base of his brain. His lifeless body fell limp on the ground.

Alejandra still had another verse to go. Renton swirled his index finger rotating his hand and encouraging her to keep singing before he disappeared again.

What happened next had the strength of a hymn rising to the heavens.

There was something about many voices in emotional harmony that was beyond what could be put into words. It brought forth the naked essence of what we are: spirit having a physical experience. And there is no dog food or cages that can change that.

"*Sólo le pido a Dios*" (I only ask of God)
"*Que el futuro no me sea indiferente*," (That I'm not indifferent towards the future,)
"*Desahuciado está el que tiene que marchar*" (Hopeless is he who's forced to go away)
"*A vivir una cultura diferente.*" (To live a different culture.)

The last part repeated the war verse and Alejandra raised her voice to a higher volume encouraging the others, so the noise would cover the silent battle that was taking place. She felt like a real ancient Shā'ir encouraging her men into battle.

When she finished, Rob played the last harmonica line with one hand while he opened the cage with the other.

It was surreal. He was there, the door was open, and *she was free*. It took her less than a second to jump on him, wrapping her naked legs around his waist and kiss him as if there was no tomorrow.

Chapter 32

Rob

Janice shrieked and moved backwards, plastering her back on the further wall of her cell when she saw Marcos opening her cage.

The man sighed and a single teardrop fell from his right eye.

"Here. I brought you some clothes."

He left the black robe on the floor and moved back and away to give her some space.

She quickly took the clothes and covered herself, but she didn't try to come out of the cage, as Marcos was at the door.

"Where is Hack?"

"On his way. We had to split up, and he took the helicopter. He is landing."

"Oh… Renton?"

"Right here," the Spartan man said and nodded.

She relaxed noticeably.

"Look. We need to talk," Marcos added.

Janice slanted her head and changed her demeanor.

"About?"

"Us…"

"There is no *us*."

"I know. That's exactly what I need you to know that I now understand."

"Oh… I'm listening."

"You are a jewel, but you are not my girl anymore. I'm not that bad myself, in spite of everything, but you will never love me. I deserve something better than living alone. We all do." She nodded, and he continued. "When your mom told me you had been kidnapped, I went crazy, but not in a possessive way. I was worried about you. That got me thinking. I do love you, you know? But it's now more like a sister, like when we were kids."

"That's how I remember you most of the time. Only you really scared me with the kidnapping."

He nodded.

"So here's my proposition: I won't bother you, but I will look after you. Think of me as your dark guardian angel."

"Does that mean I can leave the house with no fear of you kidnapping me again?"

"And go shopping and spend all the money belonging to the asshole you got yourself on black pearls."

"I heard that," Hack's voice interjected.

Marcos snickered. "Good," he said and moved away from the door to give them space.

Rob wanted to witness what was about to happen. He was a sucker for happy endings, but Renton put his heavy mass of muscles in front of him and gave him *the look*. As if on cue, Alex took his hand and pulled him to one of the lateral rooms—if you could call a tent a room. He did manage to see a bewildered Hack on his knees, holding Janice's delicate frame with reverence, cradling her in his lap with her face hidden in the curve of his neck.

"Is she ok?" Rob asked Alex.

"She swallowed the ring…"

Oh…

Epilogue

Rob

The club was dark. Candlelight pushed away the shadows just enough for people to see each other's faces at the small square tables. On a platform, red lips and dark hair, the singer was giving emotion to a tune that Rob knew by heart, with only a piano as accompaniment. A single long leg ending in a red stiletto escaped the black dress. It was *El Hombre que Yo Amo* (The man I love), a ballad Alex had chosen for him and was singing right now.

Rob walked to the bar, and around.

The bartender, Genaro, grinned and they shook hands.

"Am I the luckiest bastard on earth or what?" asked Rob, looking at Alex.

"You certainly are," the young man answered still smiling.

Rob put his elbows on the bar and they both kept religious silence until the song ended.

Applause, whistles and catcalls followed the performance, including Rob's, who just loved the freedom that living among Argentinians gave him to express his emotions unfiltered.

Alejandra climbed the bar with ease, sat with her legs hanging, and gave him a heart-stopping kiss. That position gave Rob lots of ideas.

"Mmm can I eat your pussy?" he murmured in her ear.

She smacked his shoulder and closed her legs tightly.

"Of course not!" She looked nervously at the bartender, who had moved to the furthest corner and was cleaning spotless glasses.

Rob tried his imploring face. "Please?"

"Your puppy dog eyes don't work with me." She tried to keep a straight face but couldn't, snorting unceremoniously.

He laughed with her, and tenderness showed in his eyes.

"When we get home?"

"I'd love that…" she said before going for another kiss.

"Get a room, will ya?" A very well-known voice interrupted.

"Hack? What the hell are you doing here?"

Hack was at the bar, all the way in Mar del Plata, Argentina—almost falling off the southern edge map—with a rounded-tummy Janice by his side.

"Janice? Oh my gosh! why didn't you tell me?" Alejandra climbed down the bar to embrace her friend in a bear hug.

"Congratulations, man," Rob told his brother in life and they shook hands across the bar. "Gena," Rob called the bartender. "Can you close shop?"

"No problem."

"Did you have dinner?" Rob asked Janice.

"Not yet."

"Let's go. It's on me."

Rob winked as he saw Hack's surprised expression.

"Don't get all excited. I'm taking you to see how real people eat around here."

"Not a fast food place…"

"Nah… only teens go to fast food places. They think it's cool. You're gonna love this place. They have schnitzels."

"Really?" Hack's eyes lit up and his lips pulled into a grin.

Outside, Rob almost bumped into Hubert Wilson, who was shuddering unstoppably.

"Hubert, what are you doing here?"

"Freezing my black behind. That's what I'm doing. I thought we were going to the beach!"

"We are at the beach, only it's a cold-ish one. Especially at night. Don't worry, I have another coat in the car."

They walked half a block to his Fiat Uno. Seating four people in it would've been very challenging. With Wilson, it was mission impossible, and he wasn't Tom Cruise.

Hack looked around nervously.

"Safety?"

"Just maintain a distance from spaced-out looking guys and motorbikes and you should be ok. People are very decent and friendly. Darn junkies."

Rob opened his car and retrieved a jacket. Wilson put it on immediately.

"My SUV's over there. Why don't we take it instead?" Hack said when he saw the size of the mini car.

"Ok."

Rob drove the rental around the ocean boulevard to show them the views of the bay, until the beach of Alfonsina, and then he turned to go to the place he'd chosen. It was called *Montecatini* and served pretty good seafood, plus Italian and steaks, all under one roof.

Coffee was at a different place called *El Torreón*, which gave them fantastic views of the bay and the atmosphere he liked for a good conversation.

"What brought you all the way here?" Rob asked. The girls had chosen a different table to be able to get up to speed. Wilson was at yet another table eating a dessert with gusto. So Rob and Hack were left alone.

"A check," Hack answered, and his eyes shone.

"If you want the money you gave me for the collection back, you're out of luck. I already spent most of what's left after paying my father."

Hack sighed and shook his head. "Oh, man, I should have known…"

"Hey, have some faith, will you? We bought a two-bedroom apartment in a great area with partial ocean view, the bar for Alejandra, the car you saw and a nice old house we turned into my clinic."

"Wow. I'm impressed. So no more collectibles?"

"Oh, yes. I'm getting big into local artists. So much talent. But… on a budget."

Hack snorted.

"Not funny, man." Rob laughed. "Ok, it is."

Hack smiled.

"It looks like everything is looking up."

Rob nodded.

"It is. Alex controls everything and gives me some cash to play with. Works great."

Hack smirked.

"Believe it or not, it's pretty normal around here."

"Women are in control of the finances?"

"Just the family budget for the most part, but yes."

"No shopping sprees?"

"Nope."

"Wow… Well, Janice is not big on shopping either, except when it comes to her garden. I've spent a small fortune, but it's so worth it."

Both men smiled.

"Don't you miss it? Home?" Hack asked.

"I miss… some stuff. Like having lunch with you at the golf club. I miss my car, I have to admit. Other than that, I was very alone and didn't know it. Funny enough I see my family more over here than over there. My mom is coming next week. My dad passed through last month on his way to Uruguay. Apparently, they're investing in Punta del Este so I will see a lot of my brother in the near future. And Alex's family… they are *very Italian.* You should see them. You open the door, and there's one person after another entering with lots and lots of food."

Hack chuckled. "Lovely."

"As a matter of fact, it is," Rob answered, and his eyes became misty.

"Things were too intense over there and the kidnapping of the girls was the last straw. I was sick and tired of the threats over my license for practicing functional medicine. And there's still the opioid issue in the clinic."

"My people are working on clearing that up."

"Thanks, man. It was Millicent, isn't it?"

"I'm sure she was connected, but she did cover her ass carefully. What do you want to do about her?"

"Nothing. Happiness is the best revenge."

Hack nodded. "So you're happy here…"

"Very much. Alex is just perfect for me and I'm pretty much a rock star. I even have celebrities in my clinic. And what am I doing? Same thing I was trying to do over there."

"You're doing well. Alex is a miracle worker."

"That she is."

Silence extended between them as they took in what had happened.

"Janice pregnant… Man, I can't believe you didn't tell me!"

"It was her idea to keep it a surprise. Bring the invitations in person."

"You mean she said yes?"

"Yep. She said her talk with Marcos changed everything, that it freed her. And it really did. She wasn't getting pregnant before, and two months after we arrived… morning sickness, change in eating habits, a missed period… and there it was: a baby."

Hack raked his short hair.

"You know? All the time during the rescue trip I was sure she would be a haunted shadow of herself. That we had already lost them. It's the opposite. She is like a ray of sunshine."

"Yes. She's beaming."

They both watched their women talking in a corner.

"Are you guys signing a prenup?"

Hack sighed. "Yeah. I didn't want to, but it was her main condition. She even made it sound as if she were protecting her estate from me. You should see the mischief in her eyes. Funny."

"And what was that about a check?"

"Oh. We finished the appraisal, and I sold two of the pieces to a museum. Something Egyptian looking. They were important for them, not sure why. My man smelled gold and went for it. He got a sixty million deal for the pair. I paid ten million for his wisdom and decided to split the difference with you."

"Are you serious?"

"Yep."

"What on earth am I going to do with all that money?"

"Well, you could keep investing in property. Doc Quack has a nice multilayered business going on, including vacation cabins. You could also set up a bigger budget for your collection. Evidently, you have a keen eye for hidden jewels. You could even open a gallery."

"That sounds really good."

Hack just grinned.

"Do you have any new plans?" Rob asked.

"Since we got the good news, I've been thinking a lot about the world we live in, and the world I want for my child. So I'm juggling a couple of business ideas to help steer the wheel so to speak: green rooftops with restaurants featuring Janice's recipes. Or… a health insurance company for *quack doctors* like you."

"I like both…" Rob grinned.

Behind the floor to ceiling windows, the bay reflected the lights of the ocean boulevard and the city behind it. Mar del Plata displayed its charm as a perfect background for the whispered conversation of the two sirens, each radiant in her own way.

Rob pulled his cell phone and took a picture. It was certainly a night to remember.

Dear reader,

Thanks for giving this book a try. I hope you had as much fun reading it as I had writing it. And if you didn't, well, I wish you find the books that give you what you are looking for.

If you have comments, suggestions, questions, anything, I would love to hear from you. You can contact me by email at: contact@anadantra.com

Other contact channels:
Website: AnaDantra.com
Facebook: @AnaDantra
Pinterest: pinterest.com/anadantra

See you next time,
♥ *Ana* ♥

Dear reader,

We hope you enjoyed reading *Tango With Me*. Please take a moment to leave a review, even if it's a short one. Your opinion is important to us.

Discover more books by Ana Dantra at
https://www.nextchapter.pub/authors/ana-dantra

Want to know when one of our books is free or discounted? Join the newsletter at http://eepurl.com/bqqB3H

Best regards,

Ana Dantra and the Next Chapter Team

The story continues in:
Dreams of Chuy by Ana Dantra
To read the first chapter for free, please head to:
https://www.nextchapter.pub/books/dreams-of-chuy

About the Author

Ana Dantra is a pen name. The woman behind the character is a mom of two teenagers and a cat, who lives somewhere in South America at this time. She lived in Spain for a while and the USA for several years, where she met very interesting people, both local and immigrants. Her stories are all fictitious, but the amazing people she encountered in her travels certainly planted seeds and shaped her views.

A Migrant's Romance Series

Life Hack (Book 1, Colombia)
Tango With Me (Book 2, Argentina)
Dreams of Chuy (Book 3, Uruguay)

Tango With Me
ISBN: 978-4-86750-372-0

Published by
Next Chapter
1-60-20 Minami-Otsuka
170-0005 Toshima-Ku, Tokyo
+818035793528
7th June 2021

Lightning Source UK Ltd.
Milton Keynes UK
UKHW010928250621
386141UK00001B/108